THE POWER OF ZEAL

Dawn of a New Age

By

JERMANE J. ANOYA

To
Cynthia
from Jermane!
Hope you
like it.

Book Cover Designed by
Christine M. Rinaldi

The Power of Zeal
Dawn of a New Age

v2.0

Outskirts Press, Inc.
http://www.outskirtspress.com

ISBN: 978-1-4787-1443-9

PRINTED IN THE UNITED STATES OF AMERICA

Dedications

To my friends who helped me edit my book and to my age-mates, who pushed me to have it published by constantly asking if it was finished yet.

Acknowledgements

I acknowledge the great efforts of Cristine Ranaldi who was my graphic artist. When I tried to paint a picture of what my vision for the cover was, she had the task of interpreting the meaning behind my vast, wild river of an imagination, and she couldn't have done a better job.

I'd like to acknowledge my dad who guided me through the byzantine process of book publishing every step of the way.

I want to thank my sister Amy and my mother Sandra for their support over the course of writing this book.

Lastly, I'd like to acknowledge my older brother Rocky, who wasn't directly involved in helping me come up with ideas, but taught to be spontaneous. He was the one who got me writing from the very beginning.

The Prologue of Tales

LONG AGO, IN the year 2012, my half ancestors, a race that was called "humans," discovered a then new species of life on my home planet Jupiter after finding out from years of study that it also had an inhabitable atmosphere. Of course, a large number of humans fled from Earth to this distant planet, frightened of the foreboding catastrophe that was scheduled to occur by the Mayan calendar that year on December 21st.

The plan was that if the unknown phenomenon was false, the earthlings would just fly back to their home planet, but their transportation vessel was destroyed in the landing. Fortunately, from the stories that were passed down, all passengers survived the crash. The humans would come to find that the inhabitants of this huge planet was an alien, but human featured-like race called the Eyerobis, also known as the "Eyebots" (a nickname made by humans to match most Eyerobis's rather cold exterior, making them seem like robots) or the E.B.s.

The new race (from the earthlings' point of view) was very advanced and possessed incredible eyesight which came with special power. The Eyerobis were also able to comprehend and demonstrate the art of controlling energy, like us. This species, through their evolution, learned that energy could be controlled, harnessed, and expelled in what is now called an "energy beam."

Over time, the two separate races merged into one. July 5, 2061, marked the firstborn of the fused species. This girl, maybe my great-times-one-million-grandmother, was said to be named Eyerohu because she was the first combination of Eyerobis and humans. My ancestors decided to call the mixed blood of the Eyerobi-human hybrid, the See-throughs. This new race now makes up about 70 percent of Jupiter's population, which is also the race my family and I are a part of, 20 percent makes up a race of animal-like monsters, and 10 percent is none other than the nearly extinct Eyerobis and earthlings.

Anyway, back to the past. As generations passed, the humans started to enhance and ultimately, evolve, because of an adaption they were forced to undergo. After getting used to the intense gravity difference from their previous home planet, they turned into something more superhuman, like the Eyerobis, and even more so when the capability of flight was discovered from basic energy control around the twenty-third century.

A See-through family name from the more superhuman generation, Dawn, then became famous for their exceptional abilities. Inevitably, the three races on Jupiter specialized in protecting themselves against and maneuvering around unknown catastrophes. This family became well-known for their usually shrewd combat skills, along with exceptional speed and strength.

Since the race of earthlings flew on a spaceship through Jupiter, crashing into the atmosphere, ultimately damaging it and causing harmful radiation to fly everywhere, Jupiter was without a protecting atmosphere. This harmful radiation, even though the effects went unnoticed by the three humanoid species of Jupiter, affected Jupiter's creatures in a big way. This caused them to mutate and be thrown off the course of their natural evolution. These identified creatures are called demons or monsters, but most famously, "Beings."

At any rate, without a protecting atmosphere, before long, stray meteors started to bombard the planet frequently, and this series of events was named the Asteroid Wars. The Dawn family, again, showed their awesome powers by protecting most of the planet with powerful energy waves. The asteroids stopped years later at the year of 2202 when a man from another well-known family used a new technique to put another atmosphere around Jupiter, so rocks that did start to hurtle toward the planet would burn up in the atmosphere. However, this technique shortened man's lifespan, and scientists have recently sighted stray asteroids every now and then in craters near the north.

The biggest asteroid, which was too large to be stopped, crashed, leaving a massive crater very close to Jupiter's center. The fact that the crater was created so close to Jupiter's center left the natives calling the site See-through's Core.

Insanely engrossed in martial arts and fighting, a small number of people, mostly selfish humans, started to kill their weaker adversaries and opponents. Since the habit was going on for decades now, the citizens who were against the sickening habit were found battling the killers and mercenaries in epic battles called the Slaughter Wars, which started in 2425.

The Dawn family was also thought to have battled in these low times of Jupiter's history. They, too, wanted to test their skills in the melee, but they showed a deep respect for life. Legend says that instead of killing their opponents, they gave them a second chance at life. However, if their opponents couldn't respect that, the family member would hastily finish them off.

Another family, fed up with cruelty of the Slaughter Wars, began a journey to gain a power so great, it would ultimately end it. The Zeal family was awesome in battle, but they specialized in inventing new technology. They excelled at finding new ways to enhance life for Jupiter's people, animals, and on other planets through science.

From previous research, they found out that a new element, a matter they named "zeal" after their family name, was the most powerful, energy-supplied, and purest substance in the Milky Way universe. After taking two weeks to build one, a Zeal family member named Kochin flew to planet Neptune in a high-speed spaceship, where zeal was purest, then harnessed and preserved it in a see-through, graphite orb.

When he flew in the spaceship back to Jupiter, avoiding where the Slaughter Wars were playing out, he constructed a green glass orb before filling it with a newly developed, everlasting energy technique. He also removed the zeal preserved in the graphite and placed it into the orb, fusing it with everlasting green electrical energy so the zeal's energy would never fade. This way, the gassy substance would not seep out of the orb and would be forever harnessed. The only way to be exposed to zeal's abilities is to catch a whiff of it, kind of like what prehistoric humans call "drugs." There is one side effect, though, other than having your physical and mental abilities increase by one hundred-fold. If you've been exposed to too much zeal, it puts a huge strain on your body. That's why you can only take one whiff, or you will be filled with so much energy, basically, you explode, or, the zeal will act like a poison and slowly kill your cells if you are more tolerant! Some are more tolerant to the strain than others; however, Kochin would never know about this.

Zeal is not just meant to give you power. Mother told stories about how zeal was meant to signify the Dawn of a New Age, a vague title for a long era of peace in the universe created by the youth of today. Souls were only meant to use zeal to protect themselves and others from harm and to have the power to forgive. How this legend came about, I'll tell you!

Kochin named the glass orb that was infused with everlasting energy the Zeal Orb. Then he decided he was going to find a safe place to keep the orb before exposing its values to his followers in their rebellion against the Slaughter Wars. However, as Kochin was flying away north from his home where he landed his spacecraft, he accidentally caught a whiff of the substance in his hands. He noted the very sharp pain in his nose and body before involuntarily flying at high speeds with normal effort. He quickly raced back home to tell his wife and kids about the phenomenon. He tried to demonstrate what he did, but when he took a second whiff, he collapsed on the floor. When his wife asked frantically what was wrong, he explained that he had already taken a whiff of it. Before he could further explain, he died. For future science, his wife took one whiff of the orb before her eldest son could stop her. After a minute, she took another whiff and followed the same fate as her husband. The eldest son quickly noted that inhaling two whiffs of zeal could mean certain death and headed north to find a safe place to store the orb, like his father wanted. He was forced to bring his two younger twin sisters along, figuring it would be safer not to stay in one place.

The sixteen-year-old boy's name was said to be Arcrise, and halfway through his trip, he decided that he would use the zeal first to help fight in the war. Letting it course through his veins, the zeal improved Arcrise's body mentally and physically by one hundred-fold. With his newfound strength, Arcrise spent most of his life helping to fight in the war and introducing zeal as a new element on the "Periodic Table." He also spent the rest of his teen years and adulthood introducing zeal, with his sisters, to Eyerobis, humans, and See-throughs that were on the rebelling side.

At the end of his days, old and tapped out, he built a shrine for the Zeal Orb at the far north of Jupiter where it could eternally rest, far out the reach of villains from the Slaughter Wars, since most of the battle was down south. He made it a tradition for the women in his family, starting with his granddaughter, to guard the orb, and have the men absorb the zeal's power to better help fight in the Slaughter Wars. However, before Arcrise died, he stated to his grandchildren that if any future generation members of his family declined to carry out that burden, he would respect that. But for sons and daughters that did take up the challenge, they would take turns guarding the Zeal Orb shrine from impure souls who inevitably learned about it, as he had to.

In the early 2800s, villains who were not against slaughter oddly started to grow in numbers and were starting to gain the upper hand. The younger brother of the latest Zeal Orb protector, a young See-through named Vegeta Zeal, was about to step in and even the odds. However, just before Vegeta was about to leave the shrine where he was visiting his sister for the battlefield, a pure-hearted but weak Dawn family member appeared at the foot of the shrine, being one of the few full See-through-blooded knowers of the Zeal Orb's powers. He was on a quest for power like Vegeta's ancestor, Kochin, once was, ultimately leading to the Zeal Orb's creation itself.

The seeker's name, Jaylou Dawn, was in search of more power so he could protect his family against the Slaughter Wars, since he was too weak to do it himself. When Vegeta recognized this gesture of desperation, he granted Jaylou the gift of zeal, letting him catch the Zeal Orb's scent, watching as his body enhanced. But Jaylou was not yet aware of the fact that his own body reacted to the zeal's exposure that was never recorded before.

The Zeal Orb's power dispersed through the ends of Jaylou's genetic makeup and beyond, cementing into and morphing with his blood. After the mysterious occurrence passed, Jaylou paid it no mind and declared that he was forever in debt to the Zeal family for giving him the power he needed to protect his family. This turned into respect, then trust, and then, ultimately, a long-lasting friendship.

Jaylou and Vegeta then both fought side by side as best they could to fend off foes that appeared in all forms during their day in the Slaughter Wars. By the time their generation of fighters was ready to be replaced and they hit their peak, they had reduced the enemy participant number in the war staggeringly.

Vegeta, at the near end of his life, went back to his shrine to protect the Zeal Orb while Jaylou decided to go back with him. Jaylou then cajoled Vegeta to let his family move further south to Xaphias so both their families could meet (which would start an almost, current, 8,000-year friendship), but strangely, Vegeta told his family members to watch the Dawn family for any signs of unusually powerful members that might later be born in their home in Xaphias. He ended his life with a new legacy for his sons, grandsons, and great-grandsons that would improve the future.

In the early 3050s, the Zeal family confirmed that the zeal's properties were mixed with the Dawn family's DNA from studying them like Vegeta ordered. After noticing how, when some children of Dawn family kin learned how to fight and they could open the gates to the zeal's power without even absorbing zeal from the actual Zeal Orb, there was no question. Opening the gates to the zeal's power includes: the huge power spike that sharpens your abilities by one hundred-fold, a deep, green, electrical aura circulation that forms around the body, and a side effect which turns your irises a deep yellow shade, no matter their original color.

When the Dawns started to fight in the Slaughter Wars, they showed a natural knack and exquisite talent for fighting, like most Dawns before them. With the first generation of zeal part of the Dawn family's genetic makeup, the then current Zeal and Dawn family members made and an even bigger difference by far then the members in Vegeta and Jaylou's time.

The members of the "okay-with-slaughtering" side of the Slaughter Wars were mostly Eyerobis with too much pride clouding their judgment. They wanted to gain a sense of dictatorship rather than "order" over the other species on Jupiter. However, a large portion of humans and Eyerobis following those ideals quickly started to die off.

Since the Eyerobis aged and matured much differently and were more accustomed to war than the humans, they died off much slower. The Eyerobis, with a little more than three-fourths of them fighting on the bad side of Slaughter Wars, took turns to fall back, recuperate, and harshly train. They thought they could alternate between training and fighting, so people who fought could rest and people who've been training would come back stronger. But even when they came back to fight, the difference did close to nothing. I have to admit that it was unfair for people to use zeal, but all the rebelling side wanted was for the fighting to stop as quickly as possible. Of course, whether it was right can be debated.

The war was soon ended by the now greater number of See-throughs in 3152, after more than seven hundred years of death and fighting. The See-throughs turned the war into a war against races. All See-throughs, on the good side or bad, had a vote on March 28, 3152. They wanted to elect a royal family that was well-known, rich, and would keep order on Jupiter so a war like the Slaughter Wars would never occur again.

First, they voted for the Zeal family because of their exceptional leadership skills, intelligence, and their ancestor's invention of the Zeal Orb. However, the Zeal family declined the offer because of the division among all races, physical and social division, which was the idea that was being proposed. the rest of the See-through populous was had in mind about the other races, who were their ancestors. Next, the See-through populous elected the Dawn family for their amazing strength and good-hearted judgment, but they declined the offer due to similar reasons. When the See-through race became desperate, they chose the third most powerful family, the Castellians, who accepted the offer. The oldest member, sixty-year-old Damian Castellian, would be king the rest of his life, and then his son or daughter would rule, and so forth.

King Damian established an empire and divided Jupiter into five separate lands. The land I live in is the Land of See-throughs, which is southeast. The Land of Humans is northwest, and the Land of Eyerobis is northeast of the See-through Core (people refer to places in their location east, west, north, or south away from the See-through Core which is roughly the center of Jupiter), so it makes a triangle around the center island of Jupiter. The Land of Demons or Beings was placed south of the Land of Humans, outside the triangle. The fifth section was called No-Man's-Land, which is just a large section of northern, uncharted, uninhabited islands.

Over the generations, it is thought that humans and Eyerobis established their own royal lines, but the names of them are still unknown to even my brainy mom. Anyway, the Castellian family's Imperial Guards and Knights were scattered across the globe to make sure every nation was protected from anyone or anything leaving or trespassing. That way, no one could leave their own land. Castellian Kingdom was carefully positioned and built just north of See-through's Core and has been keeping "order" for millennia. If any group of rebels challenges them against their rule, Imperial Knights have permission to execute them. Most people call rebel groups like that, a group of people striving for a well-known or common goal, a "guild." Guilds can be and have been formed by all three races at least once and tend to be made up of a mixture of races. Members are always trying to convince other people to join their group to increase their manpower.

Nevertheless, even with the new See-through empire's policy of having Imperial Knights keep order in all Lands, the Eyerobis started ambushing the other Lands in 3238. The Eyebots were much more furious with the See-throughs for casting them aside than the humans because this was their original home planet. This feud ended as quickly as it began as the Eyebots realized how apparent their own weakness in strength and numbers was. They went into hiding for about another four hundred years, seemly respecting the royal family's laws, but Mother said they were just training, waiting for the right moment to strike.

When the Eyerobis, or their bandit name, the Eyebots, came out of hiding, they were stronger than ever. The See-throughs and Eyebots met in battle in southern No-Man's-Land, while most humans were left out of the feud.

Technically, the Eyebots were much stronger than the See-throughs since they were more advanced fighters and lived longer life spans, but the See-throughs had strength in numbers. The Eyerobis still hadn't recovered due to their losses from the Slaughter Wars; that's why these epic battles were called the Last Eyebot Wars.

At the dawn of the forty-first century, the war was still filled with heated battles and sacrifice. The two sides just kept coming back stronger and stronger, like one boy trying to outdo the other. Both sides eventually learned that it was possible to draw energy from places one would never even think of, like a moon, water, a star, or even a rock! As generations passed, the battles raged on, and the war just kept becoming more complex and intricate. Later, Beings from the Land of Demons were taught how to control energy and fight as well, helping the good side as well as the bad side of the Last Eyebot Wars.

In the year of 6729, with just a little aid from the Demon race, the Last Eyebot War finally ended when the just over sixty-seven thousand pride-deprived Eyerobis retreated to their land after nearly three thousand years of destruction. The Eyerobis left the See-throughs to rebuild their land in peace. Warriors from the Land of Beings leftover from the feud have been allowed to coexist with them and live in harmony for more than three thousand years now.

As the world advanced, nations became even more secluded from each other aside from the treaty Beings have with all nations; but there has been long peace in my nation as far as I know. The locals of my town have even created an annual martial arts tournament so See-throughs could express their skills the correct way so there would never be a repeat of the Slaughter or Eyebot Wars again. The Castellian family keeps on saying they're waiting for the right moment to show peace around other nations, but they're still afraid and uncertain of the Eyebots. My mother says the next generation of heroes has to rise up to the challenge of cleaning up the ashes of the past and building a brighter future. She says that is the only way, or else we would never know what it's like to be outside our land and explore the other nations. She suspects that uneasy peace would just continue on until the Dawn of a New Age, when the nations are finally brought back together by the unwavering will of the next generation…

Enter: Jadeleve of the Land of the See-throughs

I HUFFED FRANTICALLY as I ran through a thorn-bush-infested forest, running away from my hungry pursuers. Four savage, sharp-clawed Beings hurtled themselves at me, attracted by the bag of sweet-smelling apples that I just collected. I didn't know what species they were, because after the humans came and brought some of their animal species along, they started mixing in with the mutated creatures here! Probably thousands of new species exist that scientists haven't yet named. The ecology is messed up beyond repair.

I flinched in staggering pain as my bare feet made contact with sharp thorns and sticks, but I knew I couldn't stop or my predators would slice me in two. However, I finally lost control and tripped over a log before the beasts closed in and circled around me. I had to use all my energy to stand up and face them. One by one, they lunged at me, ripping at my flesh causing blood to pour out as I shivered with agony, but hardly any regret.

"Stop it! I found these apples, so go find your own!" I pointlessly demanded, realizing I might as well have screamed at the ground. "Okay, then, I guess playtime is over."

Filled with pain and determination, my eyes started to glaze. The incredible force that was the very core of my genetic makeup was urging me to stand firmly. Green radiance started to encircle me, giving me power, making my vision even sharper, while the force was also creating harsh winds that blew my blond hair in all directions.

"You asked for it!" I bellowed, jumping up a mere twenty feet in the air with my apple bag in my hand.

"Take this!" I yelled as I fired a generic energy blast at the ground where my foes stood. The small explosion I created scared my enemies away, but it left me exhausted. After I landed back on the ground, I waited until they ran out of sight, which took quite a long time.

I better get these apples home for dinner, I thought, embarrassed with the fact that I let the beasts attack me so harshly. But I stood up straighter, tied my apple bag around my neck, and sprinted the three miles home.

Let me explain more about Xaphias, which is my home. It's pretty sweet, and my family has been living here for many generations. You see, Xaphias is a huge section of Parabola Island, which is the best place for exporting electronic goods in the Land of See-throughs. It would probably be the best place for electronics in the whole world, but the Lands haven't been in contact with each other for centuries. However, the Crescent Strait is a small collection of islands compared to the rest of this land, and Parabola Island happens to be the biggest island.

The Land of See-throughs is split into five different counties. The Celestine County, which is another name for the

Crescent Strait, the Laputa County, the Mononoke County, the Nausicaa County, and the Fantasia County. Most of the counties were named after princesses from the royal family; all but one.

Xaphias is a low-lying land in-between two stony, gray mountain ranges; it's a valley with lush forests surrounding the bottom of the perimeter. People who live in suburban homes, which are built beside the bottom of the mountains in the forests, live peacefully and quietly. Most of us are cut off from the city in more ways than one, but we've learned to thrive here in the dark, while my family regularly climbs up the mountains to pay the city visits.

Since this area holds no poor or sick, people intentionally come down here to live in quiet, even though the city is almost equally quiet despite its budding population and attractions. Given our birthright, my family was offered a home on the tallest plateau next to our sister's family house, but my mom knew the terrain and environment in the forest was better for training. We had plenty of hungry Beings down here that we could spar against, Beings that are the descendants of those who were used in the war and were allowed to coexist with us here. Anyway, back to my birthright.

The reason I was telling you about Jupiter's past and about the wars was because my family was intertwined with both, just like zeal is intertwined within me, since I'm a member of the Dawn family and the current ZP.

Something I didn't tell you is that "ZP" stands for "Zeal Possessor." Of course, since the incident with Jaylou, every member of the Dawn family possesses that energy to some extent, but people born with extra or unusual amounts are given that title.

Zeal is the most powerful element in the Milky Way. It is composed naturally of excessive and fanatic energy. By chance, this element has become a consistently present trait in my family and appears in different quantities for each member. Other then the Zeal Orb, all outside connections to it are lost, so if something were to happen to the orb, or any of the current members of my family, the most powerful substance in existence would be lost. That's currently one of the reasons Mom urges my sisters and me to train hard, so we will be able to protect ourselves if another war was to start in our time.

Just as I approached home, which was like a refuge in a dark green sea, my body started to ache again from the aftermath of my encounter with the Beings. Mom was at the front door that overlooked the grassy field of our front yard, waiting to greet me. She looked pleased by my condition.

"It looks like you got some good training in this time," she inspected me for a second, "and it seems you had to use zeal this time." She must have read my eyes, since it takes some time for them to turn back to their violet color from the golden shade the zeal's presence deals them.

"Just getting beat up is good, too, since when we recover, and our strength grows, as you know. Now you can enjoy your birthday tomorrow." Mom glanced at my sack of apples tied around my neck. I let her untie them, and then she plucked one out and inspected it. "Looks like your apple-picking skills are improving, and you're collecting the same amount in a quicker amount of time. Great job, dear. It's my turn it's get them next time."

We went inside the house and into the kitchen, where I watched her stock the apples in our turbofridge. Then I went into the wooden family room and positioned myself on a leather couch so my mom could heal me; she inherited that talent. Ninety-five percent of See-throughs inherited traits like that from the Eyerobis, mostly from mutations. We also inherited the Eyerobis's skill of energy control so we can concentrate the energy and expel it in bursts, using the energy beams in blasts like explosives. However, we mostly inherited human customs and means of trade.

Mom joined me in the wooden family room a few minutes later to perform the healing. The family room was the largest room in the house, excluding the kitchen. It had a twenty-foot long marble table in the middle where we usually ate, along with matching marble and glass cabinets that held some of our prized possessions. Except for a few rugs with symbolic patterns on them and the tan couch which was meant to lie on only for healing, nothing else was in the family room. Mom did all her healings here. But there was a catch: I had to stay perfectly still so that the procedure wouldn't be messed up. Mom inherited the "instant healing" ability from my grandma which comes from a special chemical in her eyes. It's a pretty convenient ability on a rocky planet like Jupiter which has a set stage for long-lasting wars. Although Pupil, Iris, and I didn't inherit any of her powers, we all have unique variations of our own. Anyway, once I positioned myself comfortably, I gave Mom the signal to start.

"Okay . . ." she whispered before she locked her eyes on my red gashes and my abrasion from falling. Instantly, all the pockets of blood closed up, and my scratches were healed, as if they'd never appeared.

"The healing took longer this time. Are you slipping?" I teased.

"That's the thanks I get? Just because you're turning ten tomorrow doesn't mean you get to be thickheaded! I don't see you healing anybody," she teased back. "I'll stick around while the little ones come talk to you." As she said that, I started to hear footsteps from down the hall. "They'll be here in about three, two—"

"Hey, Jadel!" Pupil screamed. As if on cue, my two little sisters crossed the boundary from the kitchen to the family room.

I should tell you about myself and my sisters before I continue. My real name is Jadeleve Byzantium Dawn, but my sisters usually just call me Jadel for short. I was born on June 21, 10100, making my tenth birthday tomorrow. I'm about three years older than the twins, so they look up to me as their role model. Even though they can use more of their hidden abilities than I can, they are aware that I am physically and mentally stronger than they.

Pupil and Iris are fraternal twins, but they look identical, with the exception that they have totally different powers, and that Pupil is half an inch taller. They're currently seven years old, born on March 30, 10103. They inherited Mom's spiky hair, but they have Dad's silver hair and bright silver eyes.

Iris's irises change colors depending on her emotions. In Mom's day, she said she came across someone else who had the same mutation, and she told Iris that when she was older that she could choose to let it happen or not. However,

Iris doesn't have much control over it yet, and the technique takes a lot of concentration, even though she was born like that. Based on what she's feeling, though, she can use different techniques that range in power, which the whole family thinks is sweet! Usually, she tends to keep to herself to practice hiding her emotions and doesn't talk much, but when she shows her true personality, she acts like Mom: sly and collected, but also kind and gentle. Plus, she's pretty sharp and tends to use her wits to win battles, which makes her a deadly tactician. She can also sense others' emotions but keeps that to herself too, thankfully.

Pupil only shows wits that surpass even her sister's when the situation concerns her, but she usually acts as thickheaded as Dad that Mom described. Mom always tells us stories (she really loves to do that) about how Pupil looks and acts exactly like a female version of Dad. She's also the big glutton in the house, which Mom describes as a "healthy appetite," but Iris is disgusted by it while I'm afraid it could turn out be a problem in the future.

The taller one out of my two little sisters has the power to dilate her pupils whenever she wants, which I think is a pretty lame power. One of Pupil's cooler abilities is that she's able to shoot golden light out of the center of her pupils which act like flashlights. Whatever comes in contact with the light could either be electrocuted, burned, or frozen, based on her intentions. Acting as an opposite to her sister, she is very sturdy and tends to use force in battle.

Iris studied my eyes, which were the portals to the soul and could be easily read. This truth is what gives Eyerobis and See-throughs so much power.

"Looks like you had to draw from the zeal, and you were inefficient about it," she mused.

"You're expelling too much energy at once," her twin added. Confused, I looked to our mother for guidance.

"They're both right, sweetie. The zeal, even though it's part of your DNA, is slowing you down. You're not strong enough to use it yet without expelling too much energy in a short amount of time. You won't be at the point where can tap into that energy and use it for long periods until you gain the stamina, which can only be reached through special training. Right now, the zeal is eating on your life force as a substitute for that stamina. If you don't gain that power while relying so much on zeal, your life span will be cut in half," Mom warned.

The news almost winded me beyond words.

"How do I gain that stamina?" I managed. Mom looked like she was lost in deep thought.

"Silver said that the more ancient Zeal Possessors found masters to help them because being in the midst of war pushed them to harness their powers quickly. If your mind and body aren't in perfect sync, even with zeal, the strain on your life span will drag you down. That's why they had to master the stamina quickly and efficiently at a young age. Otherwise, in peaceful times, like now, you usually wait until your midteens where you've gained enough experience to fight using zeal without strain. You're too young, but something tells me we don't have the luxury of time . . ." She drifted off. I hated when she did that!

"Why not?" Pupil asked, which was a good question by everyone's standards, let alone hers.

"Sorry, I didn't mean to frighten you kids, but something tells me you'll find out tomorrow, on Jadel's birthday. You guys look pretty ridiculous; I think it's time for bed!" Mom concluded.

Iris couldn't help herself, and her eyes flashed a suspicious purple. "But I'm not tired! I want to know more about how Jadel's life is going to get cut in half!"

"You need your rest if you want to get taller and not be cranky, so get to bed!" Mom wailed, mixing teasing with assertiveness. Then Pupil and Iris reluctantly left the room and went into the kitchen where the stairs that led to the bedroom hallway were. All our rooms were located upstairs and the twins shared the big room that was to the right side of mine. I heard their door creak open and slam shut after they scampered up the stairs. Then I got a strange feeling when Mom turned back to me.

"Well, pip-pip-cheerio, off to bed!" she urged. We slowly walked up the wooden steps to the hallway as well. I heard Pupil and Iris talking in their room through the door, no doubt about my recent predicament. I was usually able to take bad news lightly, but the idea of me dying before my time was unthinkable! I needed more time to train and see how strong I could get.

After we got up the stairs, Mom turned to me again, and I got the same foreboding feeling; maybe it was a new technique she developed. Anyway, it was pitch-black, and I could kind of see, but Mom didn't bother turning on the hallway lights located on the top of the stair railing since she developed a way to see through the dark like Pupil. That was selfish of her, but I didn't bother to ask her to turn the lights on.

"I'll see you in the morning, sweetie, and be ready for anything. Tenth birthdays and the first day of a season are very auspicious times. As you know, your birthday is a combination of both," she whispered. Without another word, she walked leisurely to her room at the left end of hallway.

"Good night, Mom . . ." I whispered back just before she closed her door. Then I quietly went to my room, which was between the twins' room and Mom's. I felt my way toward my golden door hinge, clasped my hand on it, and then slowly I opened my door, let myself in, and closed it behind me.

Let me tell you a little more about myself. I'm terrified of the dark; I can't see! I rely on my sight as much as a blind person doesn't. Also, I'm not a fan of the nighttime because my fear of the dark weakens my other senses, including my tolerance to pain and my immune system. I know, it could be a real problem in the future, but I like to think my power rises with the sun. Still, Mom told me that when I was around seven, the twins' age, I had to find my own way to overcome my fear, like she did when she was my age, and ever since, I've been working on the immersion technique, where I've tried to seclude myself in dark areas frequently. Even with almost three years of that, I still can't stand the dark since I can't help panicking; it's what really gave those Beings I fought earlier the upper hand. Iris described it as my one and only weakness, but just today, I found I had two weaknesses that needed to be fixed quickly, and I can't help but be a little bit excited and scared at the same time.

So far, life in the forest has been very peaceful and quiet; I mean, it's all I ever knew. The pristine air here has been keeping me and my sisters healthy and unstressed for our whole lives, and I know we should be grateful. But the truth is, we've been dying to go on an adventure that would take us across the globe with a real purpose and real problems that needed to be solved. And finally, the night before my birthday, we've been given that chance. We've spent our whole lives training just in case, and I thought it's paid off, but just today, I found out that I'm not even close to where I needed to be. I need more time to perfect my techniques and fighting style, but supposedly I don't have much time. I just didn't understand; Jupiter has been at peace for more than three thousand years!

There's one new move I've been working on that I call the Recatus blast, but I can't get it down. In order to meet my own expectations, I want to draw both from the sun's energy and from the zeal's energy at the same time, but drawing from two energy sources at once takes a lot of concentration. You see, skilled Eyerobis were able to harness any source of energy through their eyes and expel it from any other part of their body. This is called an "energy burst." Mastering how to harness different types of energy at the same time could take years, but the same fastest way to draw energy is from your own body, the method my sisters and I are used to. However, Mother said to able master the Recatus, I would have draw energy from two different sources to give it more power, enough to gather it in my eyes and then expel it from my hands. I would have to equal the abilities of an Eyerobi who has trained for at least ten years!

Since drawing from different sources gives you different results, there are an infinite number of combinations that can make an energy blast. But the difficulty of drawing from multiple sources is so frustrating to me. Mom says for that level of attack, I'd need a master like Dad did to help me.

Speaking of Dad, he left on what Mom described as a mission nearly ten months before the twins were born, when I was just two. I didn't really remember what he was like, but after all the stories Mom has told us about him, I feel like I know him better than Granny or Gramps (my dad's parents), people we visit every month! And I get this weird feeling that he's in danger and Mom is keeping in touch with him. If she was, I didn't know why she would be keeping it a secret.

Since the Dawn and the Zeal families have been buddies forever, naturally, Dad's childhood friend was Gold Zeal, who disappeared around the same time Dad did. His wife, Sapphire, has been friends with Mom since they were teenagers, too, while her children and I have been more or less acquaintances since I was six. We usually take turns visiting each other's houses once every two months, but they don't live close by. They live on one of the highest plateaus in urban Xaphias, so we have to climb all the way up. I'm not a fan of visiting them, though, partly because I hate high altitudes and because one member of their family bugs me in particular.

Unlike most people, I don't like auspicious days or moments. Sure, those times are the easiest times to draw energy from particular sources, but when I try and fail to draw energy from certain places at those times, I get even more discouraged since it just makes failure more apparent. Tomorrow would be a very auspicious day for me; usually those times opened doors for a bright future or they brought you bad luck, so I was hoping for the odds to be in my favor.

After my reminiscing, I switched on the lights (even though I could just whisper "lights" for them to turn on) and changed out of my ripped purple clothes into my fresh purple pajamas. Even though Mom could heal my wounds, only knitting could mend the tears in my clothes. Then I hopped onto my king-sized bed and rested my head on top of Ellephoranto, who was my favorite stuffed animal and my only good-bye present from Dad. Pupil and Iris also received relics of similar value that they keep to themselves, but I mostly use Ellephoranto, who is a purple female and is elephant-shaped (an ancient elephant was a huge, gray animal with all breeds of it currently extinct), as a pillow.

Before I go to sleep, let me tell more about my room. Half of the floor is made up of wooden tiles that were painted purple, and the other half is made of a fluffy, light purple rug. Windows cover the top and right walls of the room, but the glass is specially designed so I could see what's outside, but from outside the house, nothing can be seen. I keep a large, purple marble and glass cabinet, like the one in the family room, in the right corner of my room next to my door where I keep all my zeal products, which are electronics. I keep my electric drums and guitar near the windows with my music stand so I can practice. The rest of my room consists of toys and books about Jupiter's evolution and fairy tales about the royal family. I could just use my electronics to read, but this way I feel like I'm using a good amount of space in my room. Even so, I couldn't help feeling that after tomorrow, I wouldn't see my room for a while. And with that thought, I drifted off to sleep.

When I woke up from my dreamless slumber, I rubbed

the sleep out of my eyes. Then I got out from under my covers, got out of my pajamas, and got dressed in my usual purple guise: purple shorts, a short sleeve purple shirt, and purple socks. Then I scurried down the stairs to the kitchen where Mom was already making breakfast, even though it was six o'clock. Finally, I ran past Mom, past the kitchen, past the dining room where we ate, to the living room, where the big holographic TV was. The holographic TV could be used to watch television or play video games.

Like most of the other rooms, the living-room floor was made out of pure marble. Above the inactive marble fireplace was a ledge where Mom placed all of our awards and trophies from the Dojo. Many of our family pictures were there, too, including a huge one of Dad and Gold when they were just a little older than I am now, ten.

Beside the TV stood a smaller cabinet containing our video games, games that were preserved for thousands of years by a special time capsule. This type of time capsule was designed by ancient members of the Zeal family. The Zeal Capsule is a special device that keeps the games from getting outdated and unusable. Devices like this created by the Zeal family can be powered forever by using the Eternal Energy Technique only the Zeal family knows. This invention has proved incredibly useful to "time messengers" who dream of teaching their future descendants about their current time while also preserving ancient treasures from the twenty-first and twenty-second centuries. The eternal energy move is also what powers all of our electronic appliances forever. A similar electric device is perfect for very light travel and never short-circuits in the water.

I turned on the TV with the remote and changed the channel from thirty-one, to sixty-one: the news channel. The news reporter, Beef Wang, a short fellow with tan skin, brown eyes, and messy black hair, was talking about how the Castellians were keeping See-throughs who tried to escape the land prisoner at an unknown location. A similar-looking female reporter was talking about how the royal family themselves were leaving the land to investigate the other Lands and try to unite the world. But I knew they were only trying to please their citizens, since they were terrified of what the Eyerobis might do to us for banishing them on their own planet. The Eyerobis are a very prideful and scary race.

After watching some TV, I ran back through the kitchen where Mom was still cooking breakfast and listening to some music with her earphones. Then I ran down a hallway that was beside the stairs that led to the basement door. I swung open the door and scurried downstairs to the training area.

The twins nicknamed this room "The Training Chamber" (they love giving things nicknames), and it's this blinding white room, which is the size of a least four football fields, where we train to get stronger. The Training Chamber was built underground by Dad, so we had enough space for it. This huge room is also powered by zeal, so the lights never go out. We usually keep our training equipment near the stairs, so it never gets lost, because this place can be very confusing. The chamber also isn't the safest place to be, since the intense temperature variations are deadly to youngsters and you can lose your mind here easily. Mom allowed me to start training when I was five, and even after five years of doing this, I still can't be here more than an hour and a half without losing consciousness. The twins only had two years of training under their belt, and they can't be in here for more than twenty-five minutes before they start hallucinating.

The point of this chamber is to master controlling both your mind and body. Currently, normal adults can use up to 43 percent of their maximum brain capacity, and Mom's dream is to make it possible for See-throughs to use 100 percent of their brain capacity for future generations. She said that Granny (Dad's mom) believed that the more your mind and body are in sync, the stronger you become, and the easier it is stay in the Training Chamber for longer periods of time. When Dad installed the chamber, her theory was proven. It made more sense when Mom explained to me that since my sisters and I were just children, our minds and bodies were not fully developed yet; they hadn't reached their full potential. Granny said that as we got older, if we kept training, we could unlock more of our brain capacity. That's why my sisters and I train here every other day for as long as we can.

When my sisters faint, I keep sparring with Mom until I do, and then Mom carries us out of the basement. Mom said we shouldn't spend too much time here because it could stunt our growth spurts since the intense gravity would muscle us up too much, slow us down, and put too much strain on our spines, but I do my morning exercises here almost every day, and I think it's been paying off. A true master can recall any type of energy they've drawn before and use it anywhere; that's what I've been trying to master here.

After doing some basic stretches and running around the whole perimeter a couple of times, I went back upstairs and ran to the kitchen for some breakfast. Then I saw the twins had already woken up and finished their meals. You see, from the twenty-first century, See-throughs have developed a more sanitary method of eating. First, Mom cooked bacon, eggs, and prepared sliced cheese, and then she made three bacon, egg, and cheese sandwiches (classic). Next, she prepared a glass of orange juice for each of us and set aside potato wedges, my favorite food, to finish the dish. Finally, she used a food compactor, a zeal product, to shrink the molecular structure of the food.

A food compactor is a small, one-inch green pill that is designed to minimize and store food. This revolutionary invention can hold up to one hundred pounds of grub, plus the pill itself is edible; it will taste like a combination of all the contents it's holding. The idea of the food compactor was to find a quicker and more efficient way to eat food. All you got to do is tap the pill against any type of food you want to store, and it sucks the contents inside. Most of zeal products are meant to help travelers, refugees who tried to escape the land, got thrown in jail, and broke free. My friends are right to think getting thrown in jail and losing everything is unfair, and they inadvertently try to help poor refugees whenever they can, since the food compactor is great for traveling. All you got to do is plop the pill in your mouth and, *bam*, you got all the nutrition from your breakfast in one bite, your stomach avoids expansion, and your quench for food is satisfied.

After we ate, the twins and I just sat around the house for the next couple of hours. I kept pestering Mom about when I'd get my one present, but she said she'd give it to me at noon.

At around ten o'clock, I heard a shrill cry from outside

the front door.

"Open!" a masculine voice called. The voice was distorted, like it was a recording of someone.

"Should I go take a look-see, Mom?" Pupil asked in an innocent voice.

"Wait, Pupil, I know that voice! I never forget a voice, but it can't be . . ." Mom crept uncertainly to our wooden front door.

"Ruby, it's me, Gold! Silver and I don't have time so could you hurry up!" Gold's voice called.

"Gold! It really is you, then." Mom briskly swung open the door to reveal a HS, or a Holographic Satellite. The HS was projecting the figure of a tall man with a muscular build, spiky black hair, and amber eyes in front of a strange kind of terrain. Only then did I realize that the man was badly injured and the terrain must have been a battlefield.

"Gold Zeal!? The president of the S.T.Z. Corporation?" the twins shouted at the same time, interrupting my thoughts, running toward the door from the family room. Their voices were almost interchangeable yet strangely different on a deeper level I could never really explain.

"Hey, you two must be Pupil and Iris. I've never seen you guys in person." The man then turned toward me, so I too moved toward the door. "You must be little Jadeleve, and you've definitely grown and all that, but we don't have time for a reunion. Your father is risking his life out there just so I can tell you what I need to."

"What's going on? What's wrong with Silver?" Mom questioned.

"I'll get to that, Ruby, but I need to ask you a question

first," Gold said with an urgent voice.

"What is it, Gold?" Mom whispered.

"Is it true your kids know 'The Tale of the Zeal Orb'?" he asked.

"Yes, I've been rereading that same story to them for almost five years!" Mom beamed.

"Perfect. That will save me a lot of time. As you know, kids, your ancestors, even in times of war and pain, were very kindhearted people. Even though they had the capability, they could not kill or hurt unless it was absolutely necessary. When your family and mine declined offers to be the royal family since we were the first and second most powerful families in the world, the third most powerful family, the Castellians, were elected. They originally wanted to kill off all humans and Eyerobis, but our two families were able to convince the royal family to accept a compromise. Jupiter would be separated into lands, and no one would be allowed to leave their land. After hearing this story ourselves when we were just children, Silver and I were furious with the selfishness of the royal family; they were just afraid of anyone opposing them so they separated themselves from the rest of the world in rank and in stature. Knowing the Eyerobis, they were probably twice as furious with See-throughs for outcasting them on their own planet, and I can't blame them. Our ancestors weren't perfect; no race is. The See-throughs, like all people, made mistakes, but separating the land and declaring ourselves as the dominant species was our biggest one. The royal family just wasn't aware of how much pride the Eyebots have in themselves. They'd rather have themselves as the most powerful race—or destroy everything! Because of our mistakes, they've turned into purists, but it's time for your generation to help repair the balance our ancestors have wrongfully destroyed out of fear," Gold declared.

"Right, so what's the plan?" I asked. A huge part of me was terrified, but a smaller part was quite excited.

"Silver and I knew that the Eyebots would have broken the 'covenant' the royal family established three thousand years ago to stop the war already if they weren't planning a surprise attack, and our instincts were right!" Gold explained.

"What do you mean?" Pupil blurted out in exasperation. She was worried about Dad and wanted Gold to get to the point.

"The Eyebots have been developing a new energy source for about thirty years now on Saturn. Your dad and I had a bad feeling that they were up to something, so we snuck out to their land about eight years ago to investigate. They've been preparing for you, Jadeleve. It turns out that the Eyebots on Saturn have created an artificial energy source which they named 'transflare,' which is negative energy that feeds on all other types of energy sources. Anyone who has absorbed the properties of transflare is immune to any energy burst attacks, so we've been forced to resort to hand-to-hand combat and the use of weapons. Except we've been mostly ineffective since they keep us away from getting close to them when they draw from transflare to use energy beams. When their attacks come in contact with us, it sucks away our life force, so it's almost impossible to get close. I don't know how they could have possibly created a substance like this, but zeal is the only energy source we haven't used against these guys. I suspect that they only designed transflare to absorb all energies that can be drawn from a source which doesn't include zeal, technically. Even though they designed transflare specifically to counter zeal, they might not have thought of the possibility that it isn't possible," Gold mused.

"Get to the point already! Our dad needs your help!" Iris roared while her irises then shined a furious red.

"Iris!" Mom raged.

"It's okay, Ruby; she's right, I should hurry. I mean, now that zeal can only be found in the Zeal Orb after the last of it was taken from Neptune, zeal is an unnatural energy source. Since the Zeal Orb is a man-made structure, zeal can't be drawn from a natural agent of the environment anymore.

"Now listen, things can't get much worse here! The royal family knows what has been going on up here since the beginning, but they're too afraid to take a stand and help us. Silver and I have organized an army to come help us fight the Eyebots since we found out what they've been doing; we've been trying to stop them from getting back to Jupiter. Transflare ... its powers are unreal! When someone is exposed to it, they can absorb all your attacks and fling them right back at you. We've tried to use it for ourselves, but we discovered that after you draw from it, you lose control of your own will! Even though the Eyebots know this, they don't care; they're insane! The leaders of the Last Eyebot Movement don't care who they have to sacrifice. All they want is to destroy all the other races on Jupiter! The sheer chaos of all this has turned brother against brother on our side and for the Eyebots, too. Saturn is a complete war zone ...

"But listen, I made sure to call every elite, adult fighter in the land, so for the Eyerobis troops stationed on Jupiter, I left just for you kids! And don't worry; we made sure to draw all the strongest fighters here. Even so, I know the Eyebots aren't that stupid to leave their land unprotected."

"I-I don't get it. What do we have to do?" I asked.

"You and your sisters have to gather a group to travel to No-Man's-Land. After the See-through Zeal Corporation got a sample of zeal from the Zeal Orb way back to use it as a substitute for batteries for electrical appliances, which was thirty years ago, the Zeal Orb hasn't been touched. It has remained isolated in No-Man's-Land ever since then. Jadeleve, this has never been done before since it was thought to be too risky. As you know, if you are exposed to zeal twice, then you die. However, since you were born with zeal already in your blood, technically, you've haven't been exposed to it yet. If you were to travel to No-Man's-Land and acquire the Zeal Orb, your abilities would be enhanced one hundred-fold! And you would be a force to be reckoned with," Gold explained.

"But are you sure it's healthy for us to rely on zeal to solve all our problems? Are sure it's right to rely on me?" I questioned. I've always wanted to go on this type of quest, with real problems with my sisters and me as the solution, but those were just dreams I had as a little kid. We were still just children with no experience of what the world outside was like.

"Listen, Pupil, Iris, and Jadeleve, I know you girls must be scared. Heck, I'm still terrified!" Gold exclaimed. This guy had so many different personalities. "But you have to put your own personal feelings aside for the sake of Jupiter—no, the whole universe—if things go badly. And you have to realize, you guys are not alone. We've already given certain children across the globe similar messages about this plan, and you three were the last we had to inform. I've already told my family about this, too. Silver really wanted to be the one to tell you about the plan, because he wanted to see how much you've grown and because he knows I can never get to the point right away, but he's busy at the moment . . . Anyway, I know in my heart that you absorbing the Zeal Orb's power is our best bet of winning this war; it's the ultimate trump card."

"So you told everyone else the plan first before telling us? You're basically saying we don't have a choice . . ." I foreshadowed. Now that I knew what was at stake, I didn't want to go adventuring, but for some reason, that made me feel even more excited.

"Yes! Happy birthday, by the way!" Gold replied.

"Gold, tell us more about this quest. What am I supposed to do?" Mom demanded.

"Well, Ruby, the only reason we didn't call you to come fight with us was because we needed you to raise and train these kids. That's what went on with all the other See-through and human parents that had children that were too little to leave alone when this problem started. Now that Jadeleve is old enough to train herself and watch out for the twins, you can come help us fight. We need all the help we can get. Sapphire will be by sometime today to pick you up, bring you to the meeting point where any extra fighters are gathered, then Silver will teleport to Jupiter and teleport you to Saturn. All you have to do is grab hold of his hand. At that point, I'd say only about 15 percent of Jupiter's population would consist of adults!" Gold finished, and then he smiled broadly.

"How can he be so happy at a time like this?" Iris whispered in Mom's ear.

"It's just his personality," she whispered back. Then Mom turned back to Gold.

"I don't know why Silver didn't tell me about this sooner!"

"I knew it! You're always talking to Dad behind our back! We kind of wanted to see him too," I pouted.

"Silver wanted to make sure that the kids got to enjoy a taste of a quiet and peaceful childhood before they were thrust into war. He wanted to make sure you were there to take care of them without any worries. And for the children's joy, he wanted to make sure you were thrown into this suddenly, an adventure with real action, like he knew the kids would like," Gold mused. Mom blushed, but I couldn't think of a logical reason why.

"Yeah, this might be fun!" Pupil screamed excitedly. Our dreams were about to come true. Now that I think of it, I wouldn't want to help save the world any other way.

"So there you have it; it's up to the next generation of fighters to protect Jupiter. If all goes well, maybe we can unite the Lands once again, but you have to train yourselves hard if you are to overcome this new challenge. At one point, you'll have to go beyond the boarder of the royal family's range of power since you'll have to leave the Land of See-through to cross the sea. On foot, my calculations predict it would take five years for you to reach the Zeal Orb, and this is while sprinting. But going all the way on foot is impossible anyway. If you were able to master the art of flying, which isn't easy, you could get to No-Man's-Land in about three years. If you're able to get in as much training as I predict you'll get, the trip will only take a little less than two years," Gold informed us.

"Wait, why can't Dad just teleport us to No-Man's-Land in his free time with his new technique?" I asked Gold.

"We've already thought of that. It seems that Silver can only teleport to places he's familiar with. Silver recognized this flaw early when he first developed the trick, and that's why we spent the first six months of our eight-year absence traveling the world. That way, we could go almost anywhere in the blink of an eye afterward, but we never dreamed of having to go near No-Man's-Land; the place has been virtually untouched for thousands of years. You'll have to get there on your own! Besides, all of us think that this journey should be taken by you kids alone; it will be good experience."

"We understand!" Pupil and Iris beamed simultaneously. It wasn't natural how they were able to do that.

"Personally, I think it's a bit foolish for the kids to go by themselves, but if you think it's the best way, I'll go along with it," Mom confided.

"I believe that on this quest, you'll truly understand what it means to be pure of heart, and you'll learn how to trust each other with your lives. It's a very long road, so you better be prepared for the most rigorous trials you'll ever face!" Gold warned.

"Right. Thank you for the info," Mom sighed; it was her own way of saying good-bye.

"Yeah, I best be getting back to the war. Remember: true power comes from the soul," and with that, the hologram projecting Gold dissolved along with the satellite.

Zephyr and Zenon of the Land of Xaphias

"**SOOO, WHO HAS** Gold organized to come with us, Mom?" I asked.

"The twins are coming along, of course. It will be just like a family reunion," Mom beamed.

"What? Wait! Not them!" I protested. I saw Mom smirk; she knew how much I hated one of them, Zephyr.

"They live so close by, and you're already acquainted with them; plus, you're the same age. It's a perfect match!" Mom explained.

"I don't like this tradition of being friends with the Zeals. Zenon, Gold, and Mrs. Zeal are really cool, but I don't like Zephyr; you know that," I pouted.

Suddenly, Mom's expression turned hostile. "This isn't about you, Jadeleve. This about saving the world. You and Zephyr have to put aside your differences, just like Gold and Silver did." Her voice became softer with understanding. "It might be rocky in the beginning, but I think you two will become close friends."

"I hope so," I replied, and I really did. I didn't hate Zephyr at first; it's just that her personality and mine were just so different. Still, I didn't want to make an enemy out of my teammate.

"When are we going to open presents?" Pupil asked from another room.

"Soon, hunny! I have run a few errands, and then talk to Sapphire. Why don't you girls go into town and say good-bye to your friends at the dojo?" Mom suggested.

"That's a good idea," I mused.

"I'll get these errands over quick so then we can eat cake!" Mom smiled, and then she was out the door.

I went to the family room where Pupil and Iris were playing gracefully with their favorite toys. I sat on the leather couch and watched them for a few minutes before getting comfortable enough to ask them a question.

"Hey, Pupil, Iris, do you want to do some roof-leaping?" I asked casually.

"Oh, boy! Yes!!" Pupil screamed. Iris tried to conceal her excitement, but I saw her eyes flash an ecstatic shade of green. It was their favorite game from the early days of their training to leap from one house to the next. It was the quickest way to get groceries or to get to the dojo. This way, for us, was more fun and efficient, but we got in a lot of trouble for making a ruckus on top of the roofs of stores and churches, bothering shoppers or employees. Yup, we made a lot of friends by doing that (and, of course, when I say "friends," I mean mortal enemies).

Anyway, I figured since we were going away for a while, it wouldn't hurt to roof-leap one last time.

"Come on! I'll race you and Jadeleve, Iris!" Pupil hollered

at her sisters. The three of us quickly put on our combat boots and raced out the door. Then we circled around to the back of the house where the mountain base was. Finally, we started hastily climbing up the rocky cliffs toward the upper quarter of Xaphias.

It was a very cloudy day with lightning flashing in the sky, just the way I liked it. Although I hated moist weather that was also warm, today I didn't mind, because going on this quest was the best birthday present ever; I could travel the world with my sisters while fulfilling my duty to Jupiter.

While thinking about my place in the universe, I was barely conscious of my surroundings and the fact that my sisters were ahead of me now. I picked up my climbing pace until we reached the summit. Finally, the three of us climbed on top of the edge of the second tallest mountain in Xaphias with scraped hands from repeatedly touching the rugged edges of the cliff side. This mountain overlooked all of downtown Xaphias and the forest in which we lived. From here, we could see it all! Up here, I felt like I was at the top of the world. Was that how the royal family always felt? I wondered . . .

"You see Margarita's place over there? That should be a good place to start today's roof-leaping!" I directed my younger sisters.

"Right!!" Pupil eagerly shouted, being the first to get in position to make the fifty-five-foot leap. I jumped up along with my sister with Iris close behind toward Margarita's (a teenage friend of ours) roof. Then the three of us soared through the silver-colored air. Finally, in a sequence, we landed onto the first roof from the edge of the cliff. This time, our teenage friend didn't even respond to our outbursts of sound. She was either probably so used to it by now that she decided it was no use protesting, or she was just away for the moment. We knew she wasn't much of a fighter, so she couldn't have been drafted for the war, even though she was older than eighteen. It was odd how we didn't notice the population diminishing over the years so adults could help fight in the semisecret war on Saturn. Maybe it was because we scarcely visited the upper quarter and barely came in contact with our underbush neighbors. We are very antisocial so we can train in peace.

The three of us first met Margarita at a karate tournament in Grandma Bachi's dojo three years ago when the twins first started training. She had been watching our matches in the stands. Then we met her a second time when Pupil invented roof-leaping. She worked at our favorite grocery store, and we came to buy food from her when hunting season is over.

"It's weird how we're just now noticing missing people. Before we go, we should visit Grandma," I calmly suggested. We're very fond of Grandma Bachi, who was our dad's mom and co-master (Mom was our other master).

"Great idea, sis! Let's go!" Pupil hollered her consent.

We started leaping at a faster rate onto a less important variety of rooftops in a straight path, and then we started getting fancy and zigzagged between our side of the road and the opposite side's rooftops. It was inconvenient that the dojo was located at the other side of the city, literally. We had to cross this huge bridge that was located beside Moonbeam Falls. The beautiful, glistening waterfall was a huge tourist attraction. It comes from a river that flows atop Parabola Plateau. Beyond the bridge is where Grandma has lived her whole life.

After we leaped off of the last roof, we were beside the cliff where Moonbeam Bridge started. The three of us quickly ran across the bridge, catching a small glimpse of the famous, majestic, and powerful waterfall before coming to what was called East Xaphias. Besides the lower quarter where we lived, East Xaphias was the least populated part of Xaphias.

After about twenty-five minutes of walking toward the dojo, we spotted Mom coming in our direction.

"Hey, kids. I just finished talking with Bachi. I wish I had time to stay with you while you talk with her, but I have one more errand to do," she said absentmindedly and walked back to where the bridge was.

Finally, after about four more minutes, we reached the dojo. Then, Pupil ludicrously jumped onto the roof; she obviously forgot about the last time we were here, when all three of us jumped onto their roof and broke right through it. Grandma Bachi wasn't in the mood to fix the ceiling thoroughly, so she just put a flimsy piece of wood there to cover that spot just in case it rained. This was the exact spot of flimsy wood that Pupil blindly crashed into, breaking the wood easily and falling through the ceiling once more.

"Ahhhhh!!" Pupil cried as she fell the forty feet and landed on the top floor while Iris and I cautiously watched from above.

I seriously didn't know how Pupil could've forgotten about the hole in the roof and fell. I mean, Bachi even took the time to levitate up to the top roof and put a cardboard sign next to the hole that said: "Pupil, don't forget about last time!" She even added an exclamation point to it.

"Ack!" Pupil whined as the side of her neck came in contact with the tan hard marble floor (when the earthlings brought along the idea of using marble for floors, Eyerobi scientists took a liking to it. That's why many structures have marble built into them somehow; it's a part of our culture). "Why does it always happen to the seven-year-old girls?" she continued to whine, even though both Iris and I knew she was far from hurt with a little fall like that.

"You should've read the sign . . ." I muttered before I jumped down with Iris on my tail.

"Whatever!" Pupil scowled.

Tmp! Tmp! Iris and I landed in front of Grandma Bachi's desk beside a quickly recovering Pupil. I took some time to look around Bachi's familiar main office while taking the most amount of time to look at the newly painted red walls.

"Granny!! You home?" Pupil shouted, cupping her hands around her mouth.

"She's not here, girls," Sila Zeal, Grandma Bachi's best friend, replied. "She just said that today's a special day, and that you should go find her."

"Oh yeah! We should've known!" I blurted, grabbing Pupil and Iris's hands and running toward an open window.

"Thanks, Sila! Oh, and good-bye! We might not see you for a while, or ever again, for that matter," I said cheerfully.

Sila just smiled and waved good-bye; I think she knew about our situation already.

"Good-bye, Granny Sila! Take care!!" Iris turned around to yell, even though Sila, unlike Bachi, wasn't our real grandmother.

In unison, the three of us leaped through the open

window and braced ourselves for a landing. I let go of both my sisters' hands in midair. Instead of landing in unison, we landed in sequence: Me, Pupil, and then Iris.

"Frankly, we don't have time to find all our friends from the dojo. We can't go to all of their houses. We don't even know where each one of them lives. I think we should just say good-bye to Grandma Bachi. We all know where she is," I smirked slyly. The twins both simply nodded confidently in response.

The three of us ran around to the front of the building, and then headed east. After about three minutes of running, we found Grandma's secret spot, a small cave inside a mountain. Beyond this mountain were nothing but trees and grassland. At the edge of the lush forest, the landscape is swapped for a sandy beach which is complemented by a sparkling sea, meaning this mountain is the farthest eastward landmark in Xaphias. The mountain is simply called East Mountain. On the other side of the cave was another opening, where Grandma built a seaside cottage. The view there was so beautiful that it simply took your breath away.

After we finished climbing the mountain, we navigated our way through the dark cavern and found the light to the other side where Grandma Bachi's cottage home was in view. Pupil, Iris, and I expected her to be inside, but she was sitting on the edge of her seaside cliff front yard, seemingly mesmerized by the glittering waters ahead.

Grandma was the founder of Bachi Tai Chi, a dojo gym, where kids from age four to eighteen were eligible to train for tournaments. The two buildings were inspired by her, excluding the administration's office where we were earlier. The second building, named the Judo Gym Arena (but Pupil, Iris, and I call it the Judo Gym for sort), was where all the karate tournaments were held.

Coronations and tournaments are two completely different things. Each individual has his own coronation where he or she gets to test their progress and move up a belt. If the judges think you haven't progressed, no belt for you, so you have to wait at least three weeks for another chance.

On the other hand, tournaments are held every three years to test the progress of an individual against another or the progress of everyone. In the preliminary rounds, everyone is given a challenge that tests their greatest weakness. If they don't pass, they can't go on to the fighting rounds. If you win in your age division, you are awarded a trophy. The winners of each division move on to the quarter finals, the semifinals, and then the finals. The winner of the whole tournament gets a chance to visit any one of the other Lands, excluding the Land of Eyerobis, and receives a platinum trophy. Besides the chance to travel the world, to win that trophy is my life's purpose!

Anyway, the golden sunlight was starting to peek out of the clouds, and a beam shone on Granny like a spotlight; it was the perfect time to say good-bye to our elusive and beloved grandma.

As we walked over to her quietly, I recognized the figure of grandma's kitten, Toto, who rested soundly next to a bowl of unfinished milk. Toto was especially prized by Grandma because he was believed to be the last of his kind. Cats are very ancient creatures, and if they were still around, they would surely be put in a nature reserve. Iris ran over to pet him and watched in fascination as Toto's skin rustled wherever her hand swept.

Only then did I realize that Grandma was meditating with her legs crossed, and only then did she notice us.

"I've been expecting you girls," she said almost expressionlessly. I could hear the concern in her voice.

"How much did Mom tell you, Granny?" Pupil said after she looked up from Iris petting Toto.

"I've known about this secret war for over eight years, but I'm only now hearing about the deadly properties of transflare and Gold's plan for you to journey to No-Man's-Land. This is madness! However, I have total faith in you three, and we'll be cheering for you in Saturn!" Grandma assured. Her tone was lighter now with less concern. She turned to face us, and her eyes shone the rainbow colors of the valued electromagnetic spectrum. Her irises sometimes did that, but only when she was excited or happy, unlike Iris, whose eyes changed color to mirror all her feelings. Mom believes that Iris's power originated from Grandma's.

"Wait." Iris looked up from scratching Toto's ears. "You're fighting in the war, too. You're not going to aid us?"

"Of course not! I'd very much like to, but Gold said all the elite adults will be called, and I count! I'm not that old, girl," Granny huffed. I understood her position and nudged both twins to stop bugging her.

It was true, Granny wasn't as old as you'd think; she's only fifty-two, born April 6, 10058. While I'm at it, I'll tell you all you need to know about Grandma. At full height, she stands about 5 foot 10, and even though sometimes her irises are rainbow, filled with so many colors that they seem magical, they are normally silver, like the moon.

"Well, before you go, I have a tenth birthday present for you, my dear," Grandma said before reaching into her pants pocket. She pulled out a necklace with a stellar pendant attached to it that radiated all kinds of light. When I touched it, it felt cold, and for some reason, I was disappointed.

"Well, that's no fun," Grandma frowned. "It seems that the pendant doesn't react to you. Anyway, this necklace has very special properties. The pendant can repel against minor attacks, make it easier to draw energy, and best of all, this pendant will give you some artificial stamina so your use of zeal won't cut into your life span. I want you to outlive me, of course."

"Thanks, Grandma," I said halfheartedly after I took the necklace from her hand and put it around my neck. Then I felt some heat radiate from the pendant, and I felt ecstatic.

"There we go! I'd like to see your mom top that!" Then Grandma started to look a little more serious.

"I had a feeling that this day would come when you left the house on an adventure. Your mother, Sapphire, and I have been contemplating it for ten years now, but, of course, this started before Pupil and Iris here came into the picture, so originally, we thought it would be harder on you," Bachi said, first directing her words at me, then the twins, and then me again. "If you run into trouble, I'm sure you girls will be fine. But one more thing: beware of Beings and the royal family. I fear that the Castellians' long-term fear of the Eyerobis will greatly affect your quest. Be sure to wear your combat boots every day!" Grandma lectured in her signature aloof style.

"Don't worry, we won't forget," Iris confidently assured

her, which was rare.

"Be on your way then! And remember, if you need strength, just grab it from your soul . . ."

"Right!" I confided with brand-new energy. "Let's sprint home, guys. Mom will be there any minute now. Take care, Grandma. Tell Toto we said good-bye, too, when he wakes up. Oh, and thanks for the pendant; I hope it's as handy as you claim."

Grandma Bachi nodded and I could detect the pride in her eyes. I couldn't wait for us to return to her unscathed, but in this war, that was a fantasy. I would prove to my family, and to the world, that this war was pointless, that there wasn't any one race that was dominant. My new dream was to do whatever it took to bring the four Lands together.

After we finished our good-byes, Pupil, Iris, and I raced back out of the cave, down the mountain, and past the bridge. After we got off Moonbeam Bridge, we blended in with a crowd from the nearest plaza. I thought about the directions needed to get home in my head. Okay, so we were at the far side of town, so from here, home was north. It would be easy just to roof-leap to the mountainside of West Xaphias where home was just below, but I wanted to challenge myself and the twins, so I decided we would have a race through the forest to see who could get home first. I then explained my idea to them.

"Okay, now that sounds fun! It's something new, too!" Pupil replied. Iris's eyes simply flashed an excited shade of green in response.

"Yes, so we'll jump off the cliffs from here, land in the forest, and race home. You can use anything you got up your sleeve to get home first, so are you guys ready?" I asked.

This time, both twins nodded in reply and braced themselves.

"Okay! Ready . . . go!" I roared.

I rushed up a brick building that was located in the center of the plaza, and then jumped onto the roof. While there, I could visualize the vast green forest below quite clearly. Using my sharp, pop-out vision, I spotted the tallest tree in the area and leaped for all I was worth. It was a long jump so I decided to do some flips in the air, and all I could think was: *No way am I losing this race to those scrubs! Not on my b-day.*

The fall had to be at least one thousand six hundred feet, so I had plenty of time to feel the wind on my face while I flipped. But as I got closer to my mark, I straightened out. This might have been Pupil and Iris's first time this deep in the forest, but sometimes very late at night or extremely early in the morning, I sneak out to explore, so I know this place inside and out. I figured out that the tree's leaves are very good at cushioning falls; all you've got to do is land on your stomach. It's like a soft pillow!

Anyway, I landed so softly on top of the tree that I could barely hear the sound of my impact. Finally, I quickly rolled off the tree, descending about one hundred more feet before landing in the grass.

I wasn't really paying attention to my surroundings or the whereabouts of my sisters; I just knew I had to be the first one home. I felt like I needed to get to higher ground, so I decided to leap from branch to branch instead of running. As I started huffing, I could hear Pupil and Iris's laughter echoing through the bland darkness of the forest. I suspected they decided to work as a team (it was the only way those stooges would have a chance, anyway) since their voices weren't far from each other. From the sound of their voices, I knew they were ahead of me, but soon they started to come into view. Iris was leaping from treetop to treetop while Pupil swung from branch to branch.

"Oh, no, you don't!" I bellowed, refusing to lose, and then I jumped down from a branch. I used all my energy reserves without tapping into zeal (I decided not use the zeal's powers unless necessary, but it was extremely hard. It was like trying to hold back a part of myself). In raging determination, I crouched down into a squat and mightily leaped forward, reaching speeds that I learned weren't physically possible by a human long ago on Earth.

I didn't make a sound as I advanced quickly through the thick forest. I hastily left my sisters in the dust, but in doing so, I became more fatigued with every step. My breaths were getting unhealthily shorter while sweat mucked my vision. At that point I couldn't help freaking out and tripping over branches, but I always got right back up. As the harsh winds blew the water from my face and cleared my vision, I saw that I was almost home. For the last leg of the race, I decided to go back to leaping on the branches.

"A-almost there . . ." I quietly whispered against the harsh breeze on my face that almost blew me off some branches. However, right before I was home free, literally, I gave out. The wind finally knocked me off the tree just in front of the house.

"Noooooo!!" I hollered and flailed in the air as I fell. "Noooo-oof!!" I cried in pain as my neck smashed through a thick branch in midair. Finally, I landed on my shoulder, sure it was dislocated. I crawled on the ground in agony as I helplessly tried to reach the door.

"I can . . . do it . . ." I muttered right in front of the door hinge before collapsing in a heap. Luckily, the door was already slightly open since Pupil, Iris, and I forgot to fully close it when we left. A rush of air opened it ever so slightly; just enough. Now I just had to touch the floor . . .

"Home free . . ." But right before my pointer finger could come in contact with the floor . . . Pupil swooped in and kicked it away.

"Sorry, Jadel, but *we* win!" she pompously laughed. I watched in horror as Pupil and Iris simultaneously walked through the front door.

"Get up; the smell of your failure is too much for me!" Pupil jokingly insulted me as she turned her back on me.

"Ooooh! Nice one, sis!" Iris teased as she played along.

"I'm never going to lose to them again!" I roared. I picked myself off the ground and raced up to my room.

After changing, I sat on the couch in front of the TV. As I waited for Mom to come back with the reinforcements, I studied my sisters playing with each other and their toys and decided to do something productive too, like practice playing my guitar in my room.

After thirty minutes, Mom came home bursting through the door.

"I'm back! And I brought back your company!" she hollered, and I immediately ran to the front door. Mom stepped aside, and two identical twins popped out from behind her.

They both had long, spiky, black hair, but one (Zenon)

wore her hair in pigtails, while the other (Zephyr) let her hair grow out to be shoulder length. Zephyr had sparkling blue eyes with a yellow shirt, gold shorts, and yellow boots. On the other hand, Zenon had honey amber eyes with a green shirt, green shorts, and green combat boots. She completely ignored me and went in the family room to greet Pupil and Iris. I didn't mind because I completely ignored her and went for Zephyr.

"If it isn't Zephyr. My name is Jadeleve, and it looks like we'll be partners for the next one and a half," I mocked, and then crossed my arms.

"Put a sock in it, Jadelpeeve. I already know who are, no matter how much I wish I didn't. I don't care if it's your tenth birthday. You better make it bearable for me if we're stuck together until your eleventh," Zephyr shot back calmly.

"Girls, this isn't the time to fight. Who knows, you guys might be stuck together until your thirteenth birthday," Mom said while trying to suppress laughter. "Oh, and the fate of the planet rests on your shoulders, so you have to get along."

"Okay, I guess we'll have to," I gave in, already disgusted about Zephyr's stupid joke about my name. I mean, who does that? Jadelpeeve? Please. At least it rhymes, but I could do better than that.

"Oh, Jade, where did you get that stunning pendant?" Mom gasped in awe.

"Oh, this? Grandma gave it to me as a present. She said it has special properties and can even repel against minor attacks," I explained, holding up the necklace proudly.

"Is that so? Well, I think my presents will be much better," Mom sneered slyly.

Packing only took about twenty-five minutes because we took all our necessary items and stored them in a variety of compactors. We even put in a portable washing machine, stove, and shower that didn't require taking your clothes off. Our small packs, designed for extremely light travel, only consisted of compactors with labels on them. Our food supply, between the five of us, would probably last about two months. We agreed to steal any necessary items when we ran out of supplies. That meant we were pretty much set and ready to go.

We all soon gathered in the family room where Zenon and the twins were chatting. Mom had laid out my presents and a vanilla ice-cream cake on the marble table.

"Yeah! It's time to open presents," I exclaimed. Pupil and Iris appeared on either side of me while the Zeal twins and Mom stood off to my right.

On Jupiter, it was common when celebrating a birthday, your parents would try and guess what you wanted from observing your trends throughout the preceding year. You were allowed to give your mom or dad hints, too. However, some kids get frustrated when their parents don't guess right so they just ask them for specific presents. I think of Mom guessing what I wanted as a fun game, but usually if Mom doesn't guess right, we'd go out and buy what I wanted. All I was interested in this year was to find a way to meet my dad.

After everyone sang "Happy Birthday" (everyone except Zephyr, which was awkward) and ate cake (excluding everyone but Pupil and me), it was time for presents. I noticed one box was missing from before, so there were only two presents instead of three on the table.

"Open one!" Pupil hollered while Iris's eyes flashed an excited green. I immediately tore open the first present box, which was a huge, purple, lightning-shaped guitar: sick!

"Mom, how did you know?!" I shrieked excitedly.

"I always knew you wanted another electric guitar to add to your collection. Only this one is purple and lightning shaped! If you come back—'*if*'—then guitar lessons will be waiting for you. Use it as motivation," Mom smiled.

I took the comment into consideration and found in my heart that death really wasn't a problem for me, but that was the easy way out. I had to live for the people I loved, even if they died before me. Well, back to presents!

I set my new, shiny, purple guitar on the marble table and chewed into my last present. I found a black pad with a screen on top; a descendant of one of Steve Jobs's electrical appliances. I had the strangest feeling that I'd seen it before.

"It's the See-through Zeal Corporation's transceiver. I wish I could have got you a satellite so you could actually see your father, but this is the next best thing. This device can amplify your thought waves and direct them to any person you want. That way, you can have a conversation with your dad, if you're lucky. If you try it on him once, he will be able to direct his thought waves back to you any time he wants. Through this, he will also be able to sense any dilemma you are in at any time, since he has his own. Since none of us have mastered the thought transfer technique, this is close enough," Mother explained.

"Wow, that's pretty cool," Zenon said as she inspected the pad from across the table.

I was overcome with such happiness, I didn't know what

to say.

Suddenly, out of the corner of my eye, I saw Iris's irises flare red with accusation.

"You used that one Jade to read her mind and know what she wanted," Iris screamed as she pointed at the transceiver.

"Yeah, so? It doesn't change the value of the present by that much. You haven't seen your father in so long I figured you weren't really attached to the idea of seeing him. But I was just so sad last night, because I had the transceiver in my pocket when we were talking, and I knew that you were wondering about what your dad was like. I knew it wasn't that urgent, but I was so upset at the fact that I didn't know what you wanted from your body language. I almost lost the present guessing game!" Mom explained.

"So you have been talking with Dad on the transceiver, huh? That's okay. I just wanted to see in person since you hyped him up so much in your stories. But thank you for these presents, Mom, really," I sighed dramatically for emphasis. It was rare for Mom to be out of her comfort zone and try so thoroughly to defend herself.

"I'm just glad you girls have a way to talk to your dad for once. Now that I'm seeing him, I don't need the transceiver. Plus, after this war, there might not be any dad for you to talk to," Mom laughed.

"Right . . ." I hiccupped halfheartedly.

While everyone was crowding around the living room and watching TV, ready and waiting for departure, I went upstairs and put my new guitar in my room. I decided to take Mom's advice and use it as motivation to get back home in one piece. Then I dropped my transceiver in my lightweight pack and ran downstairs to join the rest of the crew.

"Okay, girls, time to leave! You all know full well that to get to the Zeal Orb, you'll have to travel off the Coast of Parabola Island at some point. The closest coastline, which is Grandma Bachi's front yard, is out of the question since the closest landmass after that is not for over eighty thousand miles, which is a distance you cannot swim. You need time to master the art of flight anyway before you can cross the ocean to the next island in the strait. So, basically, what I'm saying is: You're on your own. You have to find the most efficient route in which you are given enough time to learn the art of flight.

"Man, I should have learned how to fly from your dad so I could teach you. Oh, well! Think of this quest as a one-question math test; if don't chose the right path, you fail, and Jupiter will be taken over by the Eyerobis! So trust your instincts and don't fail! I bought an extra cake in case Pupil finished the first one. It's chocolate . . . anyone?" Mom smiled.

I then stood to face Mom from my chair. "No way are we going to fail as long as we have one another! I promise I will become the strongest in the world and save Jupiter; that is my birthday wish!"

I think Mom recognized the fiery determination in my eyes, and she nodded. I saw tears forming in her reddish-purple eyes before she gathered Pupil, Iris, and me into a big hug.

"Uh, what about us?" Zephyr barged in.

"Oh, shut up, Zephyr. I saw Sapphire hugging you before you said your good-byes. Now it's my turn!" Mom wailed without looking up from our embrace. She let go, nodded again, and tried hopelessly to regain her composure.

I wish I could shed some tears too, but I've never cried in my life! I just couldn't find the desperation anywhere in my heart. Mom said that even when I was a baby she never remembered me crying once. I was just so composed, which I take great pride in. Meanwhile, Pupil and Iris kept clutching Mom and wailing, even though she kept telling them to be strong. I looked over and saw Zephyr making faces at me, which didn't fill my heart with desperation, but just pure annoyance and rage. I didn't want to spend another second of my childhood with her!

I knew the trip would be a long one. I just hoped we could get through it. I had no other battle experience except for spars with Mom, Pupil, or Iris. Oh, and I guess some fights with wild animals and kids at the dojo. I had wanted to get as much training experience out of this quest as possible. By the time we were expected to get back, I wanted to have surpassed Mother and G.B.

"Travel safely, girls! Remember, you have to judge the right way well, because time is not on our side! Pupil, Iris, keep Jadeleve safe! Zephyr, Zenon, I'll tell Sapphire that you both left safe and sound. Also, remember your training, girls, because experience, along with determination, will be your greatest ally," Mom lectured. "And kids, in this war, if you don't step it up, you're going to get beat so bad, it won't even be funny."

I looked Mom right in the eye and said, "That will not be a problem. I absolutely will not let any adversary get the best of me! I'll master my powers, you'll see!" I roared proudly.

"You'll have to get past me first," Zephyr taunted.

"So be it."

"Now *that's* what I like to hear! Off you little fun-sized kids go then," Mother beckoned.

As the five of us, the newest descendants of the Zeal/Dawn family, rushed out the door, Mom was there to see us off one last time. Then she did the weirdest thing: she held up the present she didn't present (get it?) to me before and had me study it carefully. I noticed that the box was a little longer than the box that held my guitar. I wondered what was inside. However, I decided I that I shouldn't ask.

Mom nodded in satisfaction. "That's good judgment, Jade. Remember that at the level of power I think you will require, it will take you three years to get to No-Man's-Land, not counting how much time it will take to get back. No matter, you guys, work hard to exceed my expectations. Silver will be by soon to pick me and Sapphire up so we can help in the war, but you should get going; there's not a moment to lose! Farewell!"

The Clash of Two Titians

SOON, WE NAVIGATED our way out of the forest and left Xaphias behind us. We had to climb down some crazy steep hills, too. I've never been outside Xaphias's mountain ranges, low air supply, and high altitudes, and I felt like there was too much air around me. Zenon decided the most efficient route was going to require passing by Celestine City, the capital of the Crescent—Moon Strait. It was also home to one of the royal family's castles.

About seven thirty, we decided we should find a place to settle down and go to bed. I mean, the sky was already pitch-black, and Pupil was using her Flashlight Technique to provide as much guidance as she could.

"I think it's time to set up camp; I'm bored," Pupil whined.

"Well, if you're bored, then how about watching me and your sister have a battle?" Zephyr suggested.

"But, Zephi, Iris won't stand a chance against you! Plus, how come you're not asking me to battle?" Pupil whined.

"I meant I wanted to battle Jadel, Pupil," Zephyr explained.

"I'd love to fight you, Zephyr, but I'm kind of tired . . ." I replied.

"Too bad! I'm tired too! Look, there is no shame in losing, but there is shame in fear. Prove to me you're not as weak as you were the last time we fought!" Zephyr roared. "Prove to me you are worthy of your title . . . or my presence!"

Deep inside, I felt something twitch. The excessive raw power that I was helplessly trying to learn to control rose to the surface.

"Okay, then," I accepted. "This time you're going down!"

"Now you're talking!" She veered out of her garrulous mode, then she started to charge at me.

"Here we go! Pupil, Iris, let's get out of the way!" Zenon screamed at the twins. I caught a glimpse of Zenon, Pupil and Iris moving at an incredible speed to a safer location to avoid being caught in crossfire of the battle

When I turned my eyes back to Zephyr, she was already on top of me and delivered a hard punch to my cheek. After the impact, I felt my feet uncontrollably skid across the stone gravel that was our battlefield in way that kicked up dust. When she confronted me again, I felt a genetic impulse taking over. The material instincts were solely for battle.

Time to bust out my new move, I thought. Somewhere deep inside my eyes, I felt something turn as Zephyr jumped forward at me again. Then I looked back at Zephyr, and it seemed that time slowed down for her. I could move around at normal speed, but her moves were slowed down exponentially, which meant my new technique, which I hadn't named yet, worked! However, when I demonstrated it to Mom, I passed out after using it twice in a row. Now it just takes a lot of my energy so I decided to only use it for emergencies. The cool part about this technique is that the person you use it on isn't aware of how slowly they're moving, and they think their opponent is moving extremely fast.

Taking advantage of my opportunity, I jammed my fist into her stomach with a forceful punch. Then I kicked her down to the ground where she skidded away on her back, making painstaking contact with skin-ripping gravel. As she helplessly tried her best to mask the pain, the technique's effect faded and she could move at normal speed once again.

When she lifted her head, I looked into her eyes, and I saw the same vacant, faraway gaze that must have been clouding mine. I could feel her vigor spike with uprising energy. Her eyes lit up in an array of light to distract me. With blinding speed, she struck my shin in a brief, cursory move. Then I cocked my head up and shrieked to the heavens in a fit of agonizing pain.

"My shin has always been my most vulnerable spot. Lucky you!" I roared.

"Actually, it wasn't luck. It's because one of my powers is being able to sense out others' weak and vulnerable points!" she answered proudly.

"Ha! Your arrogance will one day be your downfall, Zephyr, unless someone beats some sense into you," I muttered.

"It's time to switch to long-distance attacks!" she screamed. "This is a new move I've been working on. It's called . . . Foveno Beam!"

She then stood to her full height and began focusing a tremendous amount of electrical energy into her hands. "Prepare yourself to feel the full extent of my powers!" she finally bellowed in the most ponderous way possible with a severe tone.

"Hey, Zephyr," Zenon called, "don't be such an anticlimactic drama queen! Jade can't counter that!"

Zephyr turned back from her sister to face me.

"Well, I guess I was wrong about you then, Jadel. Thought the Zeal Possessor would be a worthy opponent, but I guess not!" she said with a final tone, letting the beam go.

She's got me! What can I do? I fretted. The beam was too fast to dodge, and I couldn't concentrate my energy under this much pressure. But then, my heart started pumping uncontrollably. It was like I was starving and my stomach was guiding me to food, or a ghost pushed my soul out of my body and was possessing me. Or, the zeal's power was taking over my mind. I could feel a pure, ancestral pulse flow through my body and course into the palms of my hands; invincibility was within reach.

I could clearly see a field of vast, rich green energy forming a circle around me. Finally, I was able to control my own will. I cemented the pulsating essence into the single palm of my left hand. Then I screamed, "Recatus!"

Suddenly, I let a purple beam of light fly out of my hand, which was the desired effect. I had been practicing this move in secret three years with Grandma so I could have a new move to use against Zephyr.

Both attacks emanated an intense heat that would sear the skin if it came in contact with it. The force had the potential to move seas. As my beam collided with Zephyr's yellow beam, the force knocked both of us backward. It seemed as if two flashlights' beams pushed back and forth against each other. The faceoff was a stalemate; both my blast and

Zephyr's were evenly matched in force and power. So then, when we both put more effort in the attacks to try to break the tie, they exploded.

"Ahhh!!" we both screamed at the same time. We were pushed backward in opposite directions from the harsh wind our attacks caused. And the last thing I remember was the piercing noise of my back hitting a nearby tree.

"Owww," I moaned as I felt my back. I looked up from my resting place and noticed I was in the sleeping bag I had packed inside a compactor I had labeled "sleeping." I also noticed I was covered in stripes of white. Then I realized we were inside Iris's huge cozy tent, which was made of unbreakable metal on the outside and silk on the inside. She had received it on her fourth birthday when she and Pupil first started training. She sometimes used it to camp with Pupil and me or by herself in the forest.

Anyway, my portable stove was on. Zenon was cooking fish for dinner. "What am I covered in?" I asked no one in particular, just anybody who would listen.

"There's this new invention called bandages," answered Iris who was genuinely mystified.

"It isn't a new invention; pretty old, actually," Zenon corrected.

"I guess we wouldn't know since Mom can instantly heal us," Pupil bragged.

"I know that already. We've known you for four years," Zenon said as she gave Pupil the evil eye, which is a powerful technique.

"You're just jelly!" Pupil yelled.

"That doesn't even make sense."

"Ah, I ache all over! That was a really good fight between me and Zephyr. I think we bring out the best in each other's power," I beamed.

"Hey, Jadel," Zephyr called, sitting up now, "I'm sorry for what I said about you before our battle. The power of the Zeal Possessor is overwhelming!" she complimented.

"R-really?" I blushed.

"Yes, and I can't wait to crush you under my feet! I even decided you were worthy enough to be my rival. Though I'm still not fully convinced it wasn't a fluke because of the last time we fought, so you better work extra hard to assure me," she challenged.

"Whatever, man," I sighed.

"We're starting a rigorous training session tomorrow to test our skills. As my new rival, I'm counting on you to give me a run for my money, okay?" she requested.

"I don't worry about that, Zephyr. No way are you going to surpass me. I'll show you that my limitations are imaginary," I declared proudly.

After dinner, I felt that my injuries were fully healed so I took my bandages off. Then after that, I covered up in my blanket and thought about tomorrow. Today, I surprised even myself! I had no idea where that power I demonstrated came from. If I learn to gain stamina, there was no telling how powerful I could become. I could even help fight in the war without the Zeal Orb and realize my dream bringing the four Lands together again, even if it meant dominating anybody who interfered.

Competition

IN THE MORNING, I felt some crazy energy emanating from somewhere nearby. "Who's that?" I called. I was ready for a battle.

"It's just me," Zephyr answered. "Ready to start today's training?"

"Of course, I'm ready for anything!" I shouted.

"Good. From what I saw yesterday, your peak power only shows itself when you're angry or threatened. You have to learn to harness your powers. The twins are sparing each other, and I want to observe, so I guess it's you and Zenon," she concluded.

"Okay. Are you ready, Jadel?" Zenon questioned.

"Yep!" I confirmed.

"Then let's begin!" she roared before she struck against my cheekbones with two unexpected jabs. The strikes stung more than they should have because she was generating energy into her fingertips. Caught off guard, I tried to use my Slow Motion Technique so I could regain my composure, but I couldn't concentrate. With undetectable speed, she struck me with a hard side kick in the hip.

"Ouch!" I howled in pain. Then she turned around and kicked my arm two times. I staggered back, shivering with pain and remorse.

"I-I couldn't even see you that time. How did you do that?" I asked her, trying to ignore the pain.

"At will, I can make my conjunctiva expand and become external, and since it's transparent, I can engulf myself in a transparent cloak, so I can appear invisible. It helps me evade attacks or reflect them," she informed me.

"You don't say . . ." I pondered. "Well, then, now you'll have a taste of *my* powers."

This time, I was able to slow down Zenon when she tried to use her cloak again without wasting much energy, leaped forward, and squared her hard in the stomach. To my satisfaction, she staggered back and felt the pain.

"Now how in the world did you do that? You were moving at such lightning-fast speeds I could barely see you!" Zenon asked, mystified.

"It's a new technique I've been working on. For a few short seconds, I'm able to slow you down with my eyes so much that the contents of your movements can linger for unprecedented amounts of time. To you, it seems like I moved at unattainable speeds, but in reality, I made you move incredibly slowly. Anyway, you should know by now that you can't use the same move against me twice!" I boasted. Out of the corner of my eye, I saw Zephyr trying to quiet the twins down in the midst of their awe.

"We can't i-interrupt t-their fight no matter w-what," she whispered. She was quite shaken up from what I displayed, no doubt. "That's tradition."

"I sense you haven't fully mastered that move, yet, so let's see if you can slow my signature move. Choroid Gun, go!"

She emitted a bright, radiant, lime green beam from her hand. Right as she let it fly, she took precautionary measures and shrouded herself in her transparency cloak, so if I used my Slow Motion Technique again, it would be useless. Also, the blast hurtled toward me in such a brief, quick movement that I couldn't deflect it.

"Ahhhh!!" I shouted. My scream reverberated through the area. Even the sound of the explosion from the beam collision with me couldn't shield the world from my cries of pain. I was thrown against an oak tree, hard, and slid down the trunk, barely holding on to consciousness. I could hear Zenon huffing remorse and worry and Pupil and Iris stopping their brawl to see what was going on.

"Owww! Y-you didn't have to h-hit me that hard!" I cried with dread.

"I'm sooo sorry! I put too much power into it."

"Jade!" Pupil and Iris wailed while running over to me, their voices conveying worry.

"Come on, Jadel! Is that all you've got? How could you stand up to me but not Zenon? Don't tell me I was wrong about you; I'm never wrong! Look, I know by now that insult to injury for you means you must be gaining more power!" Zephyr roared. She was right, too. I felt my energy skyrocketing, but I was so banged up that I couldn't even move. Why was I the girl with all this incredible power and barely able control it? What a waste!

"Zeal Possessor or not, it still hurts. J-just give me two hours a-and I'll be fine . . ." I said as loudly as I could before

I let my golden hair fall over my face in shame.

While I was recovering, I watched the two pairs of twins cross training. Zephyr was sparring and coaching Pupil, while Zenon was doing the same with Iris. They mentioned that their technique could use a little work.

When I was sitting beside the tree, I remembered I still had the bandages from yesterday on my arms and legs, so I decided to spend part of my relaxing time removing them. As I watched the four fighting, I couldn't help getting a little excited. I had a lot of amazing competition to be the greatest fighter in the galaxy (my other dream). I was so determined to surpass them, all of them, but it wouldn't be easy unless I could learn to control my powers and master my stamina. If I wanted to learn how to control it, I would have to face a variety of people, so why not start with . . .

"Hey, Pupil, would you spar with me? You know, for old times' sake."

"Okay," she answered, a little curious.

"Why do you want to fight her, Jade? It's obvious who will win; no offense, Pupil," Zephyr commented.

"It'll be fun! One, because I want to see how much stronger she's become, and two, I learned that if I fight a series of different opponents, I can learn how to control my powers faster. It doesn't matter who wins since it's just for experience," I replied.

"Well, that's good thinking," she flattered.

"Well, thanks . . . I guess. Now, Pupil, do want to battle or what?" I challenged.

"Of course I do! Don't hold back, because I'm using full force this time!" she bellowed.

It was true that Pupil and I have fought many times back home to test each other. But this time I had a little more control over my powers, and I was able to block and dodge her attacks, punch for punch, for about an hour.

"Whoa!" Pupil shrieked, surprised that I tripped her. She landed hard on the ground, headfirst. Then she stood up, exhausted and frustrated from her helplessness in our battle.

"Concentrate, sister! Don't just attack blindly! I want you to get as much out of this as me; so get back up and try again! Show me what you've got!" I coached. And then, all of a sudden, I could sense the inexplicable power of rage flowing through her veins.

"Concentrate . . ." she whispered to herself while closing her eyes. "Concentrate . . . Focus . . . Now hone my anger into power and energy."

I became proud of her for trying a different approach while keeping a cooler head. But, abruptly, when I was caught off guard, she leaped from her spot on the gravel and slashed my cheek with her nails. Then I could feel warm, fresh blood streaming down my face after the blow, and when I tried to jump and get away, she was already behind me.

"Let me show you my ultravolley combo!" she hollered.

Pupil slammed her foot against my back with a forceful kick. Then she took advantage of my vulnerability, appeared in front of me, and high jump kicked my stomach.

"O-ow!" I shivered with malice and pain. *Wow! Pupil has this much reserved strength? Awesome! Training with her will be fun!* I thought.

"Now for the finisher!" my sister bellowed. "Sclera Blast!!" She cupped her hands together and focused blue-colored energy in the center of her palms.

I have to get used to my new technique, so why not keep practicing? I thought. I then let my eyesight turn and my ultimate power take over. My matrix soon projected the sight of Pupil moving in slow motion. When she released her brilliant blue-colored beam from her hands, I saw a slow-coming look of despair form on her face. For that moment, to her, I was moving at incredibly fast speeds, but to everyone else, it was like watching a turtle try to move through a field of cement. She was simply terrified by how fast I seemed to her.

As she tried desperately to move away, I charged energy for my next attack while her attack was still slowly advancing. When the slow-mode period was over, I was quickly able to move out of the blue beam's path and advance on a flabbergasted Pupil who was almost done recovering.

While I ran toward Pupil, I charged even more lethal, life-draining energy into the purple orb of power levitating in-between my hands. It was an attack that I only used successfully four times before.

"Recatus!" I screamed at the top of my lungs, which was necessary to properly release all the energy in my hands. With my max energy filled within the purple, radiant, and shining beam of light, I targeted and fired at my sister Pupil. "Let's if you're strong enough to deal with this!!" I huffed.

"Ahhh!!!" the seven-year-old cried as my attack was about to make contact. "No! I—won't—lose!" Then a skinny beam of yellow light shot out from each of Pupil's pupils. As the two separate strings of light came closer to my attack, they fused together to create one much-larger beam. When her veil of light collided with mine, my attack froze completely.

I nodded in satisfaction. I was familiar with her ability to do that. "Great job, Pupil. You were able to think on your feet and use the right attack! Your reflective dense technique has improved."

"Well, I've been working on it lately," she replied.

"Wow . . ." I managed to say, looking down in astonishment at my energy blast that was now a block of ice.

"Now that we're done talking . . ." she hinted before instantly appearing behind me. Before she was able to ram her knee into my back, I was able to block it.

"That's not nice, Pupil. Only scrubs do that unsuccessfully," I lectured.

After we finished the spar, it was decided as a draw, even though I totally destroyed her, and she knew it. Then Pupil went back to training with Zephyr, and I decided to train alone while Iris and Zenon continued sparring with each other. After awhile of trying to figure out a way to use my powers without cutting into my life force, I took a break for lunch. I went to the tent and opened my bag, where I pulled out my compacter labeled "food." I went outside where I threw my peanut-sized compactor on the ground and a seven foot tall fridge instantly appeared from a veil of mist. My portable fridge, like everyone else's, was fully stocked and fresh while also filled with clone foods. That's right, a fridge that never runs out of the food you like. It's easy to get in a good workout when you know food is always waiting for you.

Very few people have access to CFs since it was just invented one month ago by the S.T.Z.C. The only reason that we have it is because Zephyr and Zenon are the daughters of the See-through Zeal Corporation's founders, while Pupil,

Iris, and I are the daughters of the best friend of one of the founders.

Out of the hundreds of foods I could've chosen from, I decided to eat PBJ just for lunch.

"Hey, Jade, after you're done eating, would you battle me?" Iris asked, the brown determination in her eyes matching the tone in her voice.

"Okay, sure, sis," I replied, intrigued. "How come?"

"None of your business. I just want to see how strong you've gotten is all," she mumbled.

"So, you're saying that Pupil is teasing you for being weaker than her because of that one time you lost to her?" I deciphered.

Iris wasn't surprised about how well I knew her in the slightest. "She offended my honor, Jadel! I'll prove her wrong by defeating you!"

"Whatever. I'll spar with you if you're that determined to prove Pupil wrong," I sighed, disappointed in Iris's reason for battle, but I was reassured by the spark in her eyes. Slowly, I happily nibbled at my lunch with my mind at peace.

Right after I finished my quiet meal, I looked over my shoulder to see that Iris was walking over to me while Pupil and Zephyr were sparring again. Zenon didn't have anybody to spar with, so she was trying to figure out the best route to Celestine City on her holographic map.

"Are you ready for a battle?" Iris asked, her irises flaring brown again.

"Yes, I am. For your sake, I'll try not to hold back," I solicitously replied. I knew how angry she could get when she found out her enemy was taking it easy on her; she felt she wasn't worthy.

As we synchronized the flow of each other's battle stances, waiting for the other to make the first move, I stared intently at my little sister, quickly realizing that she would make her move.

"Argh!" Iris shrieked as she charged at me. Then with a full speed running start, she jumped up about twenty-five feet into the air and teleported behind me. But even faced with her rapid speed, I could detect her; I quickly turned around to meet her eyes.

"Hiya!" she bellowed as she started off the battle with an onslaught of lightning-fast kicks, but I successfully dodged all of them. Then I fiercely jabbed her right in the stomach, and I didn't give any opportunity for rest. I took hold of her head and slammed it down against my knee.

"Owww!" She quivered with agony. I followed up with two fierce jump kicks to her chin with force too great for even a kid of her strength to bear.

Then I felt this sharp, familiar shift. It was Iris's power level, which was rising exponentially as she recovered from my strained assault; no way could I use my full power against her or else she'd get knocked out for too long, and time isn't something we had. Anyway, then, I started to see a colorful, spiraling aura form around her.

"Ahhh!!!" She raised her voice and clenched both fists. Then, she turned from her view of the sky and focused intently on me. When she turned to me, I saw that her irises had turned a deep and intense shade of red. It was only then that I knew she was going to channel her emotions into an attack like what she was famous for.

Finally, discs made of red light formed over in front of her eyes. I could tell she was focusing large quantities of her energy there and harnessing it into lethal power. Was she trying to kill me? I wondered.

"Zonule!!" she bellowed with a "last resort" tone. She grabbed the red discs that were hovering in the air and flung both of them at me like Frisbees. At the speed they were flying toward me and the speed of their rotation, those things would've cut deep into my flesh if they made contact. This time, I decided not to rely on my Slow Motion Technique (that's what I decided to call it for now) and just evade the attack. But when I was about jump out of the way, Iris came from behind and kneed me into the pathway of her attacks.

"Ahhh!" I shouted with sheer panic. The first attack exploded from contact with me, leaving me shaken. And then, caught completely vulnerable, the second ring sliced into my right arm and then exploded, sending me battered and broken onto the ground.

"Ohhh," I moaned with pain.

"I'm s-sorry about that, Jadel . . . Did you s-see that, Pup . . .?" Iris staggered.

"Wow, Iris, you really showed me. I bet you're surprised at what you can do," I complemented. I knew I had to let her win to help her pride, since she had so much of it.

"Sure! I showed Pupil!" she roared.

I got up and brushed off just in time to see Pupil and Zephyr finish their sparring and Zenon walking over to us.

"Okay, so here's the scope, guys. Jade, you know Crossway Thirty-two?" Zenon asked.

"Yeah, you mean that really long route that goes through

Celestine City and crosses paths with Thirty-five?" I replied.

"Yeah, that's the one. Mom, Zephyr, and I used that route to go to C. City all the time, and it seems that even in this situation, Crossway Thirty-two is the best. It's infested with the greatest number of Beings out of all the other interlocking routes, which means the most training," Zenon explained. Then she took out the map from her pocket.

"You see, right now, we're on Crossway Twenty-nine, but soon, right when we pass Mountain-Edge Lake, we'll be on Crossway Thirty-two, so let's get to it," she finished.

To Encounter a Being

After Zenon announced the game plan, we put our camping supplies back into their compactors and walked northwestward for another eight hours. When we finally reached the lake, we decided it would be best to set up camp again, and then walk around it the morning.

Through the glass window at the top of the tent, daylight infiltrated my dreams. The freezing air condition inside made me want to curl back up into my sleeping bag, but something told me I should get up, even though I couldn't tell what time it was. When I looked at our surroundings, I noticed that Iris and Zenon weren't in their sleeping bags, while Pupil and Zephyr were still fast asleep.

I decided I needed a quick shower before breakfast, so I got my pack that lay next to my sleeping bag and pulled out a compactor I labeled "shower." I had everything I needed in there to wash up; my portable shower, soap, hair products, and a sponge.

When I "launched" it, which is the proper term for opening a compactor, a six and a half foot marble shower appeared out of white mist, along with my soap products.

Now, my shower is no ordinary shower. It's especially designed for travelers. The sprinkler is soundless, so it can't wake anybody up. One wall out of the shower's five walls is a removable glass door so I can get in, get out, and not have any water spill in the tent. And also, it has a drying feature that quickly dries you off afterward so you don't need a towel or even have to take off your clothes! All you have to do is give the mechanical hands the soap products, and it applies them for you! Yeah, I've been living in luxury since day one.

After a quick shower, I came out of the tent to meet Zenon and Iris. Zenon was cooking breakfast, while Iris was standing beside the lake, so I decided to greet her. When she turned, I recognized the expression on her face; grumpy understanding.

"You took it easy on me yesterday when we were fighting, didn't you?" she accused.

"Yep. I also took it easy on Zenon and Pupil," I simply replied.

"Really? You were holding back on everyone except Zephyr? Why?" Iris questioned, her eyes yellow with curiosity.

"There's no use using full strength on a weaker opponent; I'd just be wasting extra energy! Zephyr was the only one whose skills I couldn't match with using all of my power, excluding zeal," I explained.

"Wow, Jadel, you're even stronger than I thought," Iris replied in awe.

"Yes, but, strength is nothing without ingenuity or being tactical. What's important is how you use the power you obtain. Now, come on, let's go eat!" I finished excitedly.

Near the start of a quick breakfast, Pupil and Zephyr woke up and were refreshed on the plan like Iris and I were before. I found that my mind was working rapidly and my heart was racing. We were on a quest to save the universe! It seemed only now that the weight that rested upon us had fully hit me.

I concentrated and recited my position in the world. We were heading for a route that's supposed to be infested with monsters, or Beings. Creatures that were just the descendants of Eyerobi animals and the evolved forms of mutated earthling animals. Creatures that could even use attacks similar to the Recatus attack. That meant that the infestation of Beings was concentrated at one point, and their numbers became weaker on the outskirts, so there would be a few stragglers around here. That also meant we had to keep our guard up.

Then out of the blue, I knew something was wrong and sensed that the others knew it, too. "Hey! Do you guys sense that? Monster time!" Pupil wailed.

"It's time for our first encounter with a Being on this journey. Get ready!" I advised pridefully.

"Since when did I take orders from you?" Zephyr questioned.

"Never mind that; it's here," Zenon intervened.

"Roarrr!!!" the Being cried as it appeared out of the clearing.

"Whoa, what is that?" Iris gawked.

The Being was pure black with snakelike red eyes. It also came with sharp claws and razor-sharp nails on its feet. To add to my excitement, it had two horns on the tip of its head, spikes on its long tail, pointy teeth, and a twenty-foot long body.

"Remember, young ones, no one Being has a name," Zephyr pointed out.

"Enough chitchat! I've eaten, and I'm 100 percent ready to fight! Let's go!" Zenon shrieked to match the Being's roar, which was unlike her and instead, resembled Pupil.

"Attack!!" I added.

"Take this!!" Pupil yelled as she fired her brilliant blue Sclera Blast, but the monster quickly swatted her and her blast away out of the sky.

"Pupil!" I cried. On the ground she was kneeling, coughing out blood. *What a scrub,* I thought. It was all I could do to act serious and not laugh.

"You'll pay!" Zephyr joined in. "Foveno Beam!!" Her attack, in all its golden glory, struck the wicked animal right in the eye.

"Goarrrrr!!!" the monster shrieked with pain.

"Zonule!" Iris roared when she struck the other eye. But then the fiend started blindly swatting its arms through the air and eventually squared a petrified seven-year-old in her stomach with its elbow.

"Stupid Being. I wish there were more cats like Toto around," I muttered with crossed arms. Then I started quietly charging my energy while a purple aura formed around me.

"It's my turn, believe it!" Zenon joked before she followed up with four hard punches to the monster's knee, but the beast kicked her away before she could finish her barrage. She then fell to the ground laughing in spite of herself, broken and battered.

In order to become more resilient, ancient Eyebots invented the Rejuvenation Technique. Basically, after you get beat up and are healed, you come back slightly stronger. Your skin is tougher, and you become a little faster. But the bad part is that it takes a lot of energy to hold back your power; it's almost like putting a strain on your body. Luckily, it takes less effort for us now since we've been practicing.

"Hey, ugly! Over here," I mocked.

"Gaooooh!!" the demon bawled. It followed up with its claws scraping against my cheek.

"Ahhaa-rr! Is that all you've got?" I smiled while trying to conceal my anguish. I caved with pain as another fierce attack made contact with my stomach, ripping open a fresh gash of blood. Then it came from behind and stabbed my back with a sharp sting.

"ARGH!" I screamed as the monster throttled me and hurled me hard on the ground.

"Jade! You took it too far," Zephyr mocked.

"Uhhh . . ." I muttered, with my cheek on the dirt ground. My breath was becoming shallow now, and I could feel my life force slipping.

But suddenly, my heartbeat quickened. I could feel something deep inside me tick. I knew the zeal was coming, just bobbing under the surface, and I welcomed it gladly into my soul. The energy I felt was mind-boggling, a power that no one could ever fathom; not even past zeal possessors. I mean, this would be as great a time as any to practice using the zeal without putting a strain on my life span.

"Ha-ha! Ho-ha-ho-ho! Hey, ho!" I hollered with glee. First, I stared directly into the Being's red eyes, then, after my judgment, I teleported in front of the monster and shouted as loud as I could, "Recatus!!!"

"Goarrrr!!!" the Being bellowed as it was quickly engulfed in a beam of purple light.

"All right, now you're talking!" Zephyr screeched. "Take this!!" She delivered a fatal blow to the monster's chest and sent it flying away. The remains landed hard on the ground about half a mile away.

"Phew, that got me worked up! Nice teamwork!" Zephyr heartily laughed.

"WOW! Zephyr and I were the only ones to move a muscle!" I whined, and then fell on the ground in exhaustion.

"Yeah, well, we were packing up camp!" Zenon exclaimed. I looked over to see that what she proclaimed was true.

"Good, then let's keep moving," Zephyr confirmed.

After about thirty minutes, I got off the ground and nodded in agreement. I got my pack from the ground and looked onward to our next obstacle, the Mountainside Lake.

"Yeah! Onward to Crossway Thirty-two, and Celestine City!" Pupil and Iris shouted in unison. I hated it when they did that.

Princess Celestine of the Castle in the Sky

IT WAS ONLY on the night of June 30th that we reached Celestine City, but it was so worth it! I felt like I had grown almost twice as strong since we left Xaphias, and we could get around a lot quicker! At this rate, it would probably only take us four years to reach the Zeal Orb! The training was definitely needed.

Also, we didn't arrive in the condition you might expect. We arrived in tip-top shape and ready for action!

"So, Celestine City is home to one of the Castellian family's castles. And it has the stockiest security system in the Land of the See-throughs! They only allow people on transit to go beyond this city, so we'll just go on the train this time around. We need a break, anyway. They get violent and suspicious of travelers. We have to try to pass through this city without a fuss, okay?" Zenon warned.

"I heard they're not too shabby fighters, either," Pupil added.

Hmm, it could be fun to attack them and just pass through by force, but Zenon is right. It would be best to not show off. We have to use our skills only for self-defense. If it wasn't for this war, I wouldn't be here, anyway, I thought.

While I was lost in thought, I judged Celestine City's architecture against Xaphias's. It seems that it was just a collection of beautiful, white skyscrapers and streets. However, the outskirts of the city were covered with nothing but lush green trees, which was similar to that of Xaphias's ecology. Luckily, we were on high ground so we could see the whole city. Everyone seems to be out and about even at night.

"Oh, Zen-Zen, you fool," Zephyr started. "For all that you've beefed up your brain, I'm still smarter. The train station closes at ten o'clock. We can't get tickets until morning, so we should just get on Crossway Thirty and past the boarder before—"

"You're the fool, Zephi! The security here is twenty-four/seven now thanks to the royal family being here. If we try to pass and go onto C. Thirty-four, we'll just get ambushed and thrown in the dungeon. You got to think on a wider scale. We'll just camp here until morning," Zenon explained. And that was the last thing I heard before I promptly lay down on the hill where we stood and fell asleep.

I woke with a start at noon, on the first day of July. It turns out that Zenon had bought the train tickets for the one o'clock train to Greenland, which was this lush green town in the north. It was a good distance from Celestine, so we could continue traveling from there.

Everyone else was awake but me for some reason.

"You seemed tired, and we didn't have any incentive to wake you up," Zephyr explained. "It's more pleasant that way."

"Right . . . So what do we do until 1:00?" I asked.

"We could explore the town, but we have to be around the train station," Zenon advised.

"Good idea! You know what we need? Wristbands! Every professional fighter has a wristband," Iris suggested while her eyes glowed green with excitement.

"Whoa, there. We're not at Greenland yet. Anyway, we've got to use as little money as possible, even though I'm rich. We've got to use money for important things, even though we don't need money since we have the tent and unlimited food," Zephyr bragged.

"Shut up, Zephyr. Keep your voice down. Someone might hear us . . ." I fretted.

"Too late!" said a female voice. And again, it was the last thing I heard before blacking out.

"Uhhh, where are we?" I moaned. "My head hurt so much!"

"I think we're in a jail cell, but we can't break out. The bars just absorb our attacks," Zephyr answered before gesturing to my exhausted sisters.

"It seems we've been captured by the royal family's Imperial Guards and thrown in the dungeon. Only we didn't have to cross over Celestine City's boarder to aggravate them," Zenon added.

"That's because we already had motives to capture you even before you got here," whispered a familiar voice.

My head involuntarily turned toward the voice. I focused on the figure of a tall, young girl. She had sparkly, long, flowing snow-white hair with light blue eyes. She was sporting a beautiful blue dress and white boots, and, I noticed, she had a crystal attached to her forehead. She didn't seem much older than me.

"I am Princess Celestine II! And my family has been watching you for the past eight years. We know that it's because of your fathers, Gold Zeal and Silver Dawn, that Saturn is destroying itself," the girl raged.

"Wait a minute! Our dads are trying to protect Saturn and Jupiter from the Eyerobis. They're planning to wipe out all humans and See-throughs because they think we've overthrown their planet, and they're right! Your family has been treating the other races like dirt for centuries, and now it's coming back to haunt us!" Iris roared as her eyes glowed a bloody shade of red. It was the most I've heard from her at one time in a long time.

Suddenly the bar doors opened, and Celestine charged in. Then she grabbed Iris's silver hair in her hands and yanked.

"Learn your place, little girl! The Land of See-throughs doesn't need a scumbag like you shouting nonsense! The Eyebots need to quietly suck up their pride and learn that the See-throughs are the superior race! We need to keep peace and order in our great land and protect our people from war!" Celestine screeched.

"Can't you see? It's because of people like you that make the Eyebots so angry. In a way, you started this war, and you have the nerve to say it's our fault? Our adult troops on Saturn are risking their lives to protect us for as long as they can so we can get to the Zeal Orb and gain enough power to help. And you're kind of in our way," I explained.

"Celestine, we've heard that the Eyebots are remanufacturing transflare, the ancient art that can absorb any type of energy. We're on a quest to deliver it to Saturn and use its power to end the war. Now we don't have much time!" Zenon added.

"Wait," I interrupted, "transflare already existed before this war? But, your dad said that—"

"Dad doesn't know everything. After he told us his dilemma in June, I couldn't help but think that I've heard that word before, so I began studying. It turns out that this war is just a duplicate of a war that happened in ancient times with another race, similar to our story! But that's history. Anyway, the Eyebots must have revived transflare," Zenon explained.

"Zeal is the only type of energy we haven't used against them, so it's our last hope," Zephyr summed up.

All of a sudden, Celestine tensed.

"Wait a minute! If transflare absorbs energy, than does that mean that the cell bars have transflare in them? Are the Castellians working for the Eyebots?" Pupil blurted out. It all made sense!

Suddenly, the marble dungeon wall was destroyed from an outside explosion. Through the new hole in the wall I could see hundreds of Imperial Guards charging forth. It looked as if they were fighting another army.

I lunged toward Celestine so fast she got frightened and dropped Iris from her grasp. Then I became aware of green energy forming around me: the zeal. I got in my signature fighting stance.

"Tell us what you know before I kill you!!" I screamed. Then I pushed past the apparent fear in her eyes and raised a fist.

Wait, rang a low, male voice in my head. *Don't kill her;*

she's not worth it. That will only bring more chaos. She's doing this by her dad's orders. Calm down and I'll be right there.

"Whoa, who was that?" I whispered.

"Me," the same voice replied, except it wasn't in my head anymore.

I turned to see a boy about Celestine's age in front of the hole in the wall with bruises and gashes all over his body. He had spiky black hair, golden amber eyes, a white T-shirt, blue shorts, and blue combat boots. Celestine became wide-eyed, but Zenon and Zephyr seemed the most shocked to see him.

"X-X-Xaphias? Is that you? What are doing here?!" Zephyr squealed as she was overcome with joy. Both twins ran over to him and greeted him with a huge hug.

"It's been a long time, hasn't it? Somehow, I knew you'd be here," the boy exclaimed.

"Hey, guys? You know this guy?" I asked. Pupil was still red-faced at Celestine while Iris focused on what was going on outside after she was freed from her shackles. She was gripping her hair while grimacing.

"Yeah, Jadeleve. This is our older brother, Xaphias, named after Xaphias. We haven't seen him in three years!" Zenon explained. He sure did look like their brother.

Xaphias was quick to get down to business and pushed past his sisters to confront Celestine. Then he turned to me and beckoned me to stand beside him.

"Jadeleve—"

"You can call me Jade or Jadel."

"Jadeleve, I need you to understand something," Xaphias said, ignoring my comment, and then turning to back to Celestine.

"Jadeleve, is it? The Eyebots agreed to spare my family and the rest of the land if we captured you. I'm sorry; I didn't have much choice!" Celestine explained.

"You see what fear does to your mind, Jadel?" Xaphias raged. Finally I understood.

"I know you must be scared, Celetsellian—"

"It's actually Princess Celestine Anita Castellian—"

"—but don't be stupid. In the humiliated state the Eyebots are in now, I know they will double-cross you. Their whole goal is to wipe out every living being on Jupiter and start over on Saturn, so why would they spare your family? You can't be selfish and hide this from the rest of the public. You can't keep keeping innocent travelers in prison in fear of them going to the Eyerobis Land and aggravating them. Now I know why you think it's our fault that there is the war. You think it's because we aggravated them for no reason, and now they're after the whole world. But confronting them is the only way. You guys have to stop hiding in your castle and wake up!" I roared.

"Yeah, b-but," Celestine's light blue eyes started to sparkle with tears, "we don't stand a-a chance against them! They absorb all types of energy."

"That's why we're on this quest in first place! Using zeal is our best bet!" Zephyr explained.

"Then let's test it on the transflare bars!" Celestine yelled.

It was a good idea.

Celestine ran over to press a red button, and the cell bars reappeared in front of us.

"Okay, guys! Stand back! The Recatus is made from some of the zeal's energy!" I bellowed. Then I concentrated my energy into the palms of my hands and released it at the cell bars. Sure enough, the bars became dented, but they weren't destroyed.

"Wow! Well, it kind of worked," Pupil observed.

"B-but how come the bars weren't completely destroyed? I don't understand," I fretted.

"It-it must be because that attack isn't completely made out of zeal energy. Maybe it's a mix of your energy and the zeal's," Zenon pondered.

"But the zeal was built into my energy code from birth! Wow, this is confusing. At least we know there's hope," I joked.

"How can you be clowning around at a time like this? I can't put the fate of the world in your hands. I'll tell you what! I'm the only member of the royal family here at the moment, so I call the shots! If you can escape my army of Imperial Guards, I'll let you continue your journey in hopelessness, but if you can't—well, tough luck. Guards!!!" Celestine called. Then I felt rumbling like an earthquake.

"This is crazy! You're only eleven years old!" Xaphias wailed.

"It seems you wasted quite a lot of energy fighting all eight hundred of them, my love. Dance for me! Let's see if can do it again!" Celestine taunted. Then she blew him a kiss, opened the cell door, and disappeared out of the hole in the wall.

"Well," Zephyr started, "it looks like my brother has got himself a girlfr—"

"Don't say it!" Xaphias raged, and then blushed ferociously. It was the first time I'd seen him lose his cool. Then it struck me. Xaphias probably didn't have the energy to run from the guards in his state. He was the one causing all those explosions while fighting them before!

"L-listen, guys. I'm on the run while trying to destroy a small army of Eyebots that haven't consumed transflare. The reason I'm telling you this is because I think the Eyebots have followed me here! We have to get out of here as fast we can; come on!" Xaphias roared suddenly. The five of us followed him through the hole in the wall and were immediately welcomed by rampaging Imperial Knights.

It seemed that we were on a rocky plateau. Westward was one of the Castellians' huge marble castles with green grass surrounding it. When I looked behind me, above where the dungeon was, I saw nothing but sky. *This is probably a really high plateau,* I thought.

Anyway, we followed Xaphias's lead and ran to the right. The six of us were pitting against a relentless attack from the guards, and it was probably the hardest on Xaphias. We had to punch, kick, or blast anything in sight.

But then we were backed into a cliff side of the plateau and were running out of energy fast. Just when I thought we were going to have to jump off the mountain, Xaphias screamed, "Grab hands, everyone!!" Once the order was out, I immediately grabbed the hands of the two beside me, Zephyr and Iris.

Suddenly, I felt myself being quickly lifted off the ground. I looked over my shoulder and saw that we weren't standing on a high plateau, but an enormous mound of gravel that was levitating in the sky at least twelve miles up!! Good thing I didn't jump!

I also realized that Xaphias was making the five of us levitate; he could fly! Mom said that Dad and Gold couldn't even fly until they were twenty-two! Amazing! Xaphias was superstrong! He quickly brought us down to ground level at the edge of the city.

"Wow, Xaphias," Pupil started, "that was so c—"

"Argh!" Xaphias wailed in pain just after we landed. He was carrying too much weight for his injuries.

A large portion of city's people stopped what they were doing to see what all the commotion was in the castle and started pointing at us.

We have to get Xaphias out of here, fast! I thought.

"He doesn't have much energy left! Hurry up! Let's go!" Zephyr roared, and the five us carried a half-unconscious, prickle-headed boy out of Celestine City and onto Crossway Thirty-four. And so the adventure continues!

Aiondraes, the Dragon of the Uncharted Valley

THE FIVE OF us ran northwestward all the way to an uncharted place near Greenland before we stopped. We were resting by a huge lake, probably twice as big as the Mountainside Lake, but it didn't have an official name that we knew of.

Xaphias claimed that he was feeling better, but we saw that he was still in bad shape. Oh, how I wished I could heal like Mother.

"D-don't worry, guys. I have a last resort. I didn't want to have to use this because it hasn't been a week yet, but, oh well," he sighed. He reached into his pocket and pulled out a small leather pouch. He untied the string around the pouch that kept it closed and pulled out a small green bean, almost congruent to a compactor. Then, without a moment's hesitation, he plopped it into his mouth. Then, in an instant, I felt his energy replenish itself.

"Whoa, what was that, Xaphias?" I asked in horror.

"Hmmm? Oh, the thing I just ate? It was a Healing Herb, only grown in Master Dracon's garden. If you eat a Healing

Herb, your strength is fully replenished, and you don't have to eat anything for a week," Xaphias explained. "Master gave this batch to me for my mission."

"You mean *the* Master Dracon?! The one who trained our parents?" Pupil asked in awe.

"Yes. He's the one who taught me how to fly. I've been training with him for the last three years. Anyway, I just ate an Herb five days ago after I almost lost my life in a battle with the Eyebots. That's why I didn't use it before," Xaphias explained.

"Hmmm . . . I see. So now that you're part of the group for a while, tell us about yourself, Xaphias," Iris cut in.

"Well, my name is Xaphias Zeal. I'm eleven years old, since I was born on May 16, 10099. I'm about 5 foot 3. I like sushi, fighting, and traveling. I've been traveling around the land since I was four and come to visit this county every so often. And my favorite color is blue," he replied.

"My favorite color is blue, too! I like to eat food; I'm hungry. Hey, let's have dinner!" Pupil yelled. Now that she mentioned it, I realized I hadn't eaten since yesterday.

"I could just give you a Healing Herb, Pupil. Your stomach will be bloated for—"

"I want real food, not a bean!" Pupil wailed.

"Yeah, Xaphias. Plus, you have saved those herbs for something important," Zenon pointed out.

"I guess. The good news is, I don't have to eat for a week, so I'm going to bed," Xaphias yawned.

However, right at that moment, a typhoon appeared over the lake with a small earthquake following suit. Then, I could make out the figure of an eight foot long creature fly up through the twister's funnel. As soon as the creature was above the swirling mass of water, it stopped, but that was the least of our problems. The monster was flying at high speed toward us.

"Why do we always run into Beings near lakes?" Pupil raged.

This was like no Being I had ever seen. It was aqua blue with sparkling scales all over its arrow-shaped body. It had one silver horn on the tip of its head. I realized quickly that it was a dragonlike creature with a six foot wing span, a two foot long spiky tail, with razor-sharp claws and teeth. Also, it had reddish-gold eyes that seemed to be filled with pain.

It's one of the smallest Beings I've ever seen! I thought. *It has to be just a baby.*

Soon, the dragon Being landed on the ground next to us, shrieking shrilly. Was it . . . crying? Xaphias seemed captivated and lost in thought just like I was.

"Let's attack from above! Take this!" Zephyr charged. She delivered a fierce triple kick, and Zenon followed up from behind with a hard dropkick to the dragon's forehead.

"Aiyyy!!" the Being shrieked, and I couldn't help but think it wasn't because of the attack.

The two of them attacked with deadly accuracy and lethal force.

"Eoiyyy!!" it kept crying with fear in its eyes. It just wasn't fighting back. I felt so sorry for it, but I just stood there frozen in place like a statue. Then, just like before, Xaphias's voice was in my head.

You get where I'm coming from, too, right, Jadel? I just don't feel right attacking this particular Being . . .

"Guys, stop. This dragon isn't fighting back! It's not like all other ones we've faced. What's the point of attacking? It won't fight back. This guy is just a baby," I screamed.

"Huh?" Zenon exclaimed, turning back to look at the dragon. "You're right. I just thought we were dominating him, but he wasn't even fighting back!"

"Just think, this dragon is too afraid of us to even know his own strength. I think he has great potential. I say we take him along with us," Xaphias suggested.

"That's a great idea. I think he has a good heart," I added. Out of the corner of my eye, I saw Iris's eyes turn a deep shade of green. She was on board.

"Yeah, but . . . what does he even eat?" Zenon asked.

"People food! We can give it anything in the fridge to try since we have an unlimited amount of food," Pupil suggested.

"Yeah, we have a pet dragon!" Zephyr inappropriately cheered.

"Oh yeah, Xaphias, you must be super strong. How about we battle sometime?"

"S-sure," he stuttered. He seemed embarrassed, too.

"First things first: we've got to name the dragon," Zenon declared, and then crossed her arms, lost in thought.

"We're sorry about that," Pupil apologized.

"Aiiyou!" the Being wept with forgiveness.

"Hey, can you understand us?" I questioned.

"Aiaaa," it nodded with reply.

"That's sick!" Pupil clapped her hands with delight. "Do want to travel with us? You'll get to battle a lot." The dragon nodded again. Either it actually understood us or nodding was the only conversational skill it had.

"Aiyyaa!" he screeched again. Unexpectedly, he flew around in a circle, and then tackled Xaphias.

"Argh! Of course!" Xaphias wailed after he fell down.

"Hmmm . . . I got it! We should call him Aiondraes!" Iris shouted suddenly.

"That's the perfect name!" I agreed.

"I wonder where you got *that* name from," Zenon said sarcastically.

"You're just jelly," Pupil accused.

"Yeah . . . I think you need help, Pupil. Anyway, Aiondraes and Xaphias have inspired me to learn how to fly; the five of us can't slow them down on our travels. So, as we travel north, we have to stick to a fierce training regimen. Xaphias, you will teach us how to fly!" Zenon roared.

"Okay, okay, sis," Xaphias sighed after he recovered from Aiondraes's tackle.

"Yeah! If we're going to stand a chance against those Eyebots, we're going to have to train hard," I added excitedly. I had two opponents to train with now.

"Okay, back to traveling business. The map says that we should travel north for one hundred and twelve miles on Crossway Thirty-seven. We have to go straight through C. Thirty-nine, Forty, and Forty-two. At the end of Crossway Forty-two, there is a small sea. That will take us to the last island of the Celestine County. Full Moon Island is the smallest island in the whole strait. After we pass that, we will be entering the Laputa County. I think we'll be there by July 25th. The closest town is Alamos town," Zenon explained the plan.

"Wow, sounds like you have this all figured out, Zenon!"

I crossed my arms, impressed.

"Tomorrow, the next step in our training begins!" Zephyr said.

"Right!" we all agreed, except Xaphias; it wasn't his style, so he just nodded. Aiondraes screeched instead of nodding, though.

"Yeah, let's set up camp and then eat!" I yelled. A new chapter was turning in the quest to obtain the power of zeal!

The Art of Levitation

"YOU ACTUALLY HAVE to focus your energy on the ground if you want to levitate off it, or at least that's what Xaphias said," Zenon whispered.

"Yep. You have to concentrate your energy on your feet and use the force like a rocket to fly. Once you master the technique, then you can fly smoothly and effortlessly," Xaphias himself added from his smug resting place under a tree.

"Can't we do this another time? I'm tired!" Pupil whined. Zephyr, who was helping Zenon teach the class because Aiondraes and Xaphias were too lazy, lost her temper.

"Hey, squirt, do you want to learn how to fly or not?" she yelled at Pupil, who was her own pupil and trainee.

"Yes, but from someone who can actually fly, like Aiondraes! Plus, I'm so tired, you woke me up at 6 A.M.," she countered.

"Well, we have to get an early start on training so we can fly in the future and get to our destination faster!!" Zephyr yelled again.

"The faster we get this over with, the better, so stop with

the interruptions," Zenon concluded.

"OK . . ." Pupil sighed, then sulked in defeat. "We've been training like this for the past week while traveling. I guess it took its toll on everybody. The worst part was that we didn't have time to celebrate the Fourth of July."

After about two hours of practicing the flying technique, an excited, happy voice cried, "Time for breakfast!!" I quickly recognized the voice as Pupil's.

After we set up camp and got out our food compactors, I set up a bunch of random food in front of Aiondraes so I could see what he liked to eat. First, he sniffed around the pile, and then he just started stuffing his face with whatever was in his way.

"That's quite an appetite you have there, Aion," I . . . complimented. "Yeah," I complimented. Or maybe commented? Whatever. It was lucky we had unlimited amounts of food.

After a long-awaited breakfast, it was time to pack up camp and head north. Our goal today was to reach Alamos town and sleep in an inn for a change. Aiondraes and Xaphias decided to fly ahead, leaving just the five us to run like the good old times.

After about five hours, when I started to run out of breath, I tried to take my mind off my fatigue by thinking of other things. I wondered how the "secret" war was going on Saturn. I thought about the whereabouts of Celestine after our little scrape. And I thought what good time we were making on our quest. Only three weeks had passed since we left home, and we've almost mastered the art of flying. Mother and Father would be so proud. Just thinking about warm and fuzzy thoughts like that made the running just a little easier.

"Time for lunch!" Pupil again yelled, this time wanting lunch.

"How come it's always you who asks for lunch first?" Iris sighed, exasperated, but Pupil just giggled in reply.

Right after lunch, it was time for training once again.

"You ready to train, Aiondraes?" I asked my new Being friend.

"Aioyyy!" he replied, and then once more with greater determination.

"You know the drill, guys; concentration formation!!" Zephyr and Zenon concurrently screamed like identical twins should.

The effort was strenuous, and this time Xaphias didn't even give us pointers. By focusing energy at the soles of our feet and pushing off the ground, kind of like push off the ground to ride a bike, we should've been able to fly already. But the amount of energy it takes to get used to the technique is what was delaying us. It would take weeks to get used to.

After about an hour of this, I was getting frustrated and angry. Then I decided I was going to tap into my life force energy: the zeal.

I will master the art of levitation today! my conscience bellowed. My mind and body were now one and the same. I could feel the powers of resolve, rage, bliss, fear, all the emotions I ever knew, being dispersed everywhere. Then my mind took hold of the feelings only the zeal represented: heart, soul, freedom, righteousness. And I focused those feelings into fuel. I could blast off into the sky! I could feel myself rising above the ground; above my limitations. I would surpass all those who defeated me!

"Guys, look!! I'm levitating!!!" I shouted with triumph to all my teammates.

"Whoa!! What's your secret, Jadeleve?" Zephyr blurted out.

"I don't have a secret; just find your own way! I think the experience is different for everybody," I replied.

I practiced how to elevate a little higher off the ground. I needed to learn how to float for longer periods of time without wasting energy. After another hour, I could fly pretty smoothly . . . until my concentration was broken by a shrill noise, and I came crashing to the ground.

"O-okay. I think that's enough for today," I moaned in exhaustion.

"I did it!" Zephyr also laughed in triumph, clenching her fists like she won a prize.

"Cool, you mastered the levitation. I think I should rest now," I confirmed my rival's achievement.

"You better watch out, Jadeleve Dawn, because the next time we spar, I'm going to mop the floor with you!" she declared.

"Yeah! You're on, and all that corny, rivalry junk only happens in anime," I replied. I was actually really excited that I had someone as dedicated as Zephyr to compete against, but I was so tired right now, I just wanted to take a nap.

"I'm a contender, too!" Zenon intervened. We looked over and saw that she was floating in midair. I welcomed the fierce look in her eyes.

"Hmmm. Good job, sis, but I think I'm still stronger

than you. Anyway, now that the three of us can kind of levitate, only Pupil and Iris need to learn it," Zephyr said while crossing her eyes.

"Twins, get over here! The sooner you learn how to fly, the sooner we can cross the sea!" I concluded.

The Battle between Jadeleve and Aiondraes

"WE FINALLY DID it!!" Pupil exclaimed in an otherworldly show of excitement. Iris's eyes shown indigo with fiery passion.

"Yeah, and it only took another eighteen hours," I sighed huffing heavily.

"You guys kept us up all night, but it was worth it, because now we can cross the sea. We're making excellent time on this quest! But now we should probably practice some more, and then get more rest, because we can't stop flying in the middle of the sea," Zenon explained calmly. I understood. But it was only then that I realized that Xaphias and Aiondraes were still asleep.

After a very slow breakfast (we didn't want to cramp out at sea), I went over to wake Aiondraes up, but decided to leave Xaphias be. I let him help himself to anything in my unlimited food supply fridge, and then got down to business.

"Okay, Aiondraes! Now that I know how to fly, it evens the odds if we fight. Can you spar with me?" I pleaded.

"Aioyya!" he replied, and then nodded his head.

"Great! Now, I'm not going easy on you just because you're a baby lake dragon," I spat. Then I put my serious face on and got in my fighting stance. Aiondraes then positioned himself in a counterstance: oh, it was on!

"Do you have to fight Aiondraes right now?" Zenon whined. She was still eating breakfast.

"There's no better time! I'm not waiting until we get comfortable on Full Moon Island to prove that he's a peon!" I retorted. The desired effect: I enraged my dragon friend.

Aiondraes had the first attack. He swiftly flung his spiky tail at me, which I was able to catch where there were no spikes. I tried to yank it from under him so he'd lose leverage, but he wasn't having any of that. He caught me off guard and doused me with fire. I could tell he cut back on the power so it wouldn't cause me serious damage, but the pain was still present.

While I was trying to shake it off, the dragon then doused me with a blast of freezing water, pushing me back a good one hundred meters. The mix of being hit with fire and water consecutively left my skin irritated and raw. It was so annoying and painful! I couldn't help scratching.

Aiondraes decided to take advantage of my stress and flew toward me at breakneck speed. He lashed his tail out at me one more time, but this time I was able to limbo under the strike. When he tried again, I jumped into the air to evade. Then I decided to go on the offensive and tried to kick his head with a mighty roar, but he caught me off guard with a swift strike of his claws against my face. The cut wasn't deep, but the gash came with warm blood. Debilitated, I did a double backflip before banging my head against the ground.

"Either Jadel sucks or we've got a very strong ally on our team," Zenon whispered.

"I heard that! You come try fighting him! If I can't touch him, there's no way you could stand a chance against him!" I retorted.

"Hey, I beat you once before," Zenon shot back smugly.

"Well, that was a long time ago, Zenon. I know we're friends, but the only one I will ever except losing to right now is your sister," I concluded. This silenced her and brought an understanding smirk from Zephyr. Then I turned back to the fight.

"Aioyyy!" Aiondraes bellowed. He was raring to go for round two.

Okay, I thought. *I'm using almost all of my power, so if I want to win, I'm going to have to catch him off guard.*

"Get ready, Aiondraes," I warned.

"Aioyyy!!" he beckoned. Yes, he was getting cocky.

I was prepared to use the slowdown technique. However, right before I could, Aiondraes shot gushing water all around. At first I thought it was an attack, but then, I saw him blasting his fire breath in the air where water was falling. This created blinding mist, which he blew toward my direction, incapacitating me. He was the cleverest and most resourceful fighter I had ever seen! And he was just a baby!

I used the Slow Motion Technique anyway and tried to run around the mist to catch him, but he was nowhere to be seen. I thought he might have been hiding in the mist cloud, but when I used energy to blast through it, there was nothing there. And the slowdown time was over—oh, man! I looked behind me just in time to see a fireball hurtling toward me, but I managed to deflect it away with a plain energy blast; it was strangely weak, though.

By the time I realized it was a diversion, it was too late. Aiondraes rammed into me from behind, scraping the sharp edges of his right wing against my left arm. It was a ballistic searing pain that I'd never felt before! I would never have had time to prepare for what happened next if I didn't shake off the pain as quickly as I did.

Actually, I still wasn't fully prepared. I blindly punched and kicked whatever was in front of me, but Aiondraes just blasted me away again with what felt like hydrophilic acid against my skin. I needed to turn this around.

"Okay, Recatus!!" I roared. I didn't know enough attacks to trick like Aion; that's why it was so hard to fight him. But I had to try.

After I fired my attack, I circled around and tried to get a good view of Aiondraes. I had to get up close for me to have any chance. But he had disappeared again! Now this was one sly dragon. Quickly I turned around and saw that he was on top of me. This time, I fired at him too quickly for him to dodge. Cleverly, he flapped his wings against my attack to cushion the blow. He thought he was safe for now, so he let his guard down, which was exactly what I wanted. I flew up, and then jumped right on top of him. To set up my new combo, I had to use the slowdown technique. Then, while on his back, I gathered every ounce of strength in my body and fired the Recatus at his back, cruelly. Then, before my eyes, a small explosion engulfed my dragon friend.

I thought I was victorious, but suddenly, there was this searing pain in my back. Somehow, Aiondraes had come from behind and sliced his spiky tail into my back. He kindly pulled it out quickly, though. Now this pain was like no other. It was like crystal cutting into the bones of your flesh. I needed some way to protect myself against his attacks. Then I remembered: my birthday pendant! I had kept it in my pocket since right after we left Xaphias since I didn't want any advantages over my opponents. How could I have forgotten about it when I remembered to switch it into a different short pocket on days we did laundry? Anyway, this was a perfect time to test it out.

I quickly reached into my short pocket, brought out the hot, white pendant, and put it around my neck. It would soon be time to use my newest technique.

Then, Aiondraes shot boiling hot liquid right at me. This was my chance to test out the pendant, so I didn't move. I figured right after, I would just take the pendant off. But I was guessing Aiondraes thought I would dodge his attack, so when he appeared behind me, he was bewildered. First, I bombarded him with a barrage of hard kicks and punches to his stomach, and then got back in front of his blast. The pendant, indeed, absorbed some of the attack's force, but I still catapulted backward. True to my word, I jammed it back into my pocket and both of us, Aiondraes and I, recovered quickly. But we were both running out of energy, me more than him. My blast when I was on top of him just didn't even the score. I had to use my new move to catch him off guard. But first, I had to tap into the power of my ancestry.

Suddenly, green blazed all around me. I could feel myself, mind and body, lifting off the ground.

My strength was elevating. Then, hastily, I rushed to

engage Aiondraes in combat.

"Yeah, this is where the battle gets good! Go, Aiondraes!" Pupil roared.

"Now, I'm not sure who will win at this point . . ." I heard Zephyr whisper. I really had to bring the fight now!

Aiondraes tried to keep the fight long range by blasting water right at me. I dodged the heart of the attack with a quick aerial twist, but I do admit some water got on me. But too late did I realize Aiondraes's plan: It looked like he had a new move he was keeping under wraps, too. He sent an electrical current through the air which made lethal contact with me. I let myself be shot down from the sky, but anticipated his next move: the final play. It was time to bust out my move.

Aiondraes sent his fire breath chasing down after me once I hit the ground hard. But a split second before impact, I used my new technique, the After-Image Technique.

You see, using the After-Image Technique, I could give the illusion that I was in one place, but I was really in another. It's quite simple: I just used the zeal to amplify my speed. It was a spin off the slowdown technique, with the same concept.

Anyway, while Aiondraes flew toward the spot where "I" was and lashed his tail at my After-Image, I got up really close behind him and charged up for my final attack. By the time he realized it was a fake, it was too late, and I roared.

"Recatus!" A sonic boom was followed immediately after I released my charged up energy at Aiondraes. Just like he did, I only used enough energy to knock him out and not cause any serious damage. Nonetheless, my attack did its job and knocked my dragon friend to the ground. Except for Xaphias, the rest of the posse rushed to his aid. Xaphias was crossing his arms and looked up at me with shining eyes of interest.

I was victorious! I had won! My mind raced. *I'm about to faint!*

Time for Departure

IT WAS ANOTHER two hours before Aiondraes and I were both in tip-top shape for the flight to Full Moon Island. We had packed up camp and were ready to run to the shore for launch.

"Hey, Jadel, the way you handled that fight was pretty amateurish, but you won all the same. I'll be looking forward to fighting you," Xaphias informed me, than he calmly walked away. *Just like his sister,* I thought.

Thinking of Zephyr, she walked up to me next while I was organizing my compactors within my purple pack.

"Like Xaphias said, Jade, except I don't care how you fight to win. It doesn't matter if you look cool during battle or not, because I'm going to beat you down all the same."

"We'll see about that. I'll tell you what, Zeph. Once we get settled on Full Moon Island, we're going to battle so hard, I'll show you how much the gap in-between our power has widened," I boasted.

"Hmmm . . ." Zephyr replied. She seemed lost in thought as she walked back to where Zenon was on the preparation grounds. I decided to talk to the other twins.

"So, Pupil, Iris, are you both ready for departure? You better be prepared because stopping in the ocean is scrubby!" I remarked.

"Sure, do-dad! Riddle me this! Sometime . . . Molly Malone . . . tomorrow, at three pay-am," Pupil replied.

"I think you need help, Pupil," Iris intervened.

"Wait; there actually might be something wrong with her!" I screamed. I was about to shake her to death when she raised a hand to stop me.

"Guys, I'm okay! I was just trying to tell a joke; I didn't mean to scare you. Anyway, Iris and I are ready to go," Pupil responded as calmly as could be.

"Good, but that was the worst joke *I've* ever heard," I sighed.

"Are we ready to go?" Zenon cut in.

"Y-yes," I responded.

"Great! Aiondraes!" Zenon called. Aiondraes immediately got up from his resting place while proving his quick reflexes. *Hmmm, how to train a dragon,* I thought. *Good movie.*

It took the seven of us about thirty minutes to find the shore of Earth's Sea, which was the name of this particular waterway. The shore was very rocky and secluded by tropical trees; I kind of felt at home. Finally, the sun was setting when we reached the water's edge.

"Hey, uh, guys, do want to wait another morning to fly across Earth's Sea? It's getting kind of dark . . ." Zenon whispered.

"Good question, sis. I think we should go today, though; we're already a day behind schedule. We could be at Full Moon Island by morning," Zephyr spoke.

"Hmmm . . ." It was all Xaphias added. I could concur by now that he wasn't much for speaking his mind.

"Aionyy!" Aiondraes screeched. He seemed up for our first long flight challenge.

"I get where you're coming from, Aion. I'm just saying that it would be better to go when we have full strength, but if you're up for the challenge, I'm not going to stop you," Zenon sighed.

I looked to Xaphias, the eldest, for guidance, but he was just staring blankly out at sea. *Who is this guy?* I thought.

"R-right. We should get this over with today. Who knows how much time we have before the invasion starts. The adults can't hold off the Eyebots forever with normal weaponry, so let's get a move on," I concluded.

"That settles that," Zephyr conceded, and so the race across Earth's Sea had begun.

The Tales of Earth's Sea

EARTH'S SEA WAS much wider than I expected. I thought we'd be on Full Moon Island before twelve A.M., but we were still flying endlessly long past three in the morning. Luckily, we found a very small island on which we could rest. The island that was not deserted, but it wasn't on the map. The population must've been about ten.

An elderly man with red hair and green eyes was there to greet us from his front lawn.

"You guys, except for the dragon, look familiar. What are you doing around these parts?" the man asked.

"Well, ummm . . . We're on our way to Full Moon Island. You see, we're on a quest to find the Zeal Orb so we can gain power and help fight in the secret war on Saturn," Pupil explained.

"You didn't have to give away our whole life's story, dummy!" Iris scowled.

"Yeah, it's the truth. We're just here to rest because we've been wasting all our energy flying," Xaphias summed up.

"Yes . . . I know you guys! You're the fiends who caused all the commotion I heard about at Celestine City, minus the dragon," exclaimed the old man.

"Yeah, he's new," I explained before petting Aiondraes to comfort him. He wasn't good with new people, which I found out with the travelers we had met throughout the quest.

"Anyway, I'm sure I've seen you before in person, or older versions of you. My name is Mr. Greenfield. Does that ring a bell?" he asked.

"Uhhh, well, sometimes my mom used to tell us stories about a woman named Emerald Greenfield who didn't change her maiden name. Are you related to her?" I questioned.

"Yes, yes! Emerald is my granddaughter. I haven't seen her in two years since she went to Saturn to help in the war you're talking about. She's quite the fighter. Also, she was friends with some people named Ruby Dawn, Silver Dawn, Sapphire Zeal, and Gold Zeal. I think they're all at war," the old man explained.

"Sapphire and Gold, those are our parents!" Zephyr gestured toward Xaphias and Zenon.

"Yes, I see the resemblance, with your spiky black hair. These look-alikes definitely take after Silver, and the purple and gold-haired one is the spitting image of Ruby. Hey, everybody, come on out! It's the next generation of fighters come to save us!" Mr. Greenfield roared. The expected population of ten, actually eleven, plus Greenfield, gathered in front of our posse.

"Don't worry, folks, the Being is friendly. We give you our blessing on your perilous quest. Might I ask your names before you go?" Greenfield asked.

After a long conversation about the derivations of each

of our names and our eye color significance, it was time to go.

"Wait, I have a question," Iris said.

"Yes, Iris?" a young woman who went by Lillian replied.

"Hey, you know my name because I told you. Yeah! Anyway, why are you guys awake so early?" Iris asked.

"Oh, that's because we're nocturnal! We've all developed this trait so we can work on the crops or go out at sea at night, and sleep during the day to escape the summer heat," Lillian explained.

"I would never be able to do that; I hate the nighttime. I'm a summer person; my birthday is on the first day of summer," I explained.

"Aionyyonii!!" Aiondraes screeched.

"He's right, we have to get a move on, guys," Xaphias beckoned.

"I'm tired," Pupil yawned.

"Come on, we'll have plenty of time to rest on Full Moon Island. You have to learn how to power through in times like this. Just in case, however, you should stay close to me," I lectured.

After another thirty minutes of preparations and saying our good-byes to our new allies, it was time to set out once again. At about six A.M. we were ready to go.

"Hey, Jadeleve, I hope you really can put an end to this war! Go get them, you guys," a man named Ethan encouraged.

"Right! Let's go, team!" I chanted.

"Since when did I start following orders from you?" Zephyr raged through gritted teeth. Someone didn't get enough beauty sleep.

"Come on, Zeph. We have to leave sometime anyway,"

Zenon pointed out. And with that, the seven of us set out over the high seas again. *Ha, seven seas.*

I admit the wind that was roaring in my ears was kind of soothing, and I almost drifted off to sleep a couple of times. Pupil and Iris were playing rock, paper, and scissors in midflight. Zenon was double-checking the map. Xaphias and Zephyr were sparring while keeping up with us while Aiondraes decided to go for a swim instead of flying. He was much faster in the ocean. Meanwhile, I was practicing how to sustain my ancestral powers. The zeal was becoming more difficult to activate as the flight wore on; I was losing energy. Zenon sensed my dilemma and started to worry.

"Don't worry, Jade! We'll be on Full Moon Island's Crystal Beach in about one hour!" she screamed over the wind.

Another hour? I thought. *It would be easy breezy for me to deactivate the zeal's straining energy and fly normally, but I had to gain more stamina. I had to power through!*

In the middle of my inside battle of will, a piercing cry ripped right through my thoughts. It was Aiondraes!

"Aiondraes! Can you hear us? Come out of the water!" Xaphias roared. On his command, Aiondraes shot out of the sea like a rocket, similarly to when we first met him in the uncharted valley lake. He was accompanied by at least five others of his kind that were twice as big as him.

"Whoa," Pupil stopped her and Iris's game, "are they our allies?" It was very good question, but by how freaked out Aion was, I was guessing no.

"Aiooyyyyy!!!" The five dragons cried in unison, making Aiondraes flee at full speed toward Full Moon Island. They were chasing him!

“We can’t let Aiondraes join your team, since he’s already part of ours,” I exclaimed, knowing that they could understand me. My speech must have ticked them off in some sort of way, because the next thing I knew, the biggest one had whipped his spiked-up tail against my stomach. Excruciating pain was accompanied by my backflip into the water, and my blood left a trail. Sea creatures from all over started to encircle me, which was beyond creepy.

I dealt with the pain from the strike and exhaustion from the flight accordingly. As I watched from underwater the fight between the dragons and my quest mates, my friends were getting pummeled. Even Xaphias was having a tough time. Now that I was currently out of commission and Aiondraes had fled in fear, it was five against five: a fair fight. But in my book, there was no such thing as fair!

I decided to launch a surprise attack, the slowdown technique. I made it so everybody, except the dragons, could move at normal speed. It was time for the second phase.

I flew straight up through the water, activated the zeal mode, charged up Recatus, and released at the five, all in four seconds. The five dragons had to have been blasted at least one mile away and were no danger to us now.

“Wow, Jadel! That was awesome!” Pupil squeaked.

“Come on! We’ve got to catch up to Aiondraes and get to Full Moon Island!” I bellowed. With that, the six of us quickly regrouped and charged forth.

Crystal Beach, the War Zone of Full Moon Island

"IT TOOK FOREVER to find Aiondraes," Zephyr huffed.

"I think it took longer to calm him down," Zenon added.

"I'm hungry," Pupil whined, and then her stomach rumbled for evidence. However, I think she trained herself to do that.

"Oh yeah, that reminds me. After we eat and get a good amount of rest, it's on to sparring. Who am I going to battle first?" I asked. Then I looked from Zephyr to Xaphias.

"What about me, Jadel?" Zenon said through gritted teeth.

"I didn't promise to battle with you like these two, but I suppose I can use you as a warm-up," I replied.

"Never mind . . ." Zenon sighed. "I'll go get out our capsules."

"You shouldn't belittle her; you're not that much stronger than her," Xaphias exclaimed.

"Yes, but I want a real challenge. I would accept fighting either you, Zephyr, or Aiondraes," I retorted.

"Don't get ahead of yourself, Jadel, because when I beat

you down, your pride will be hurt as well," Xaphias replied calmly, which put me in an uncomfortable position.

I was just about to retort again when he interrupted me. "You shouldn't be reluctant to fight weaker opponents, because strength doesn't always win the fight; judgment does. Judgment has the power to take the soul of any fighter. Why, I remember when I was at your stage in my career, but Dracon beat it out of me—hard. With the right training and motives, a weaker opponent can beat a stronger one any day. I hope you keep that in mind when we fight," Xaphias whispered, and then went to help Zenon get out the camping capsules.

"Sure . . ." I replied. I had been getting ahead of myself lately. Taking charge and getting cocky. I couldn't become arrogant like the Eyerobis; I had to keep a blank head.

Xaphias's talk really hit me hard, but it made me realize something: I was only human. Well, I had partial human DNA. Even though I hated the sound of humans from stories that were passed down, some had very strange straights similar to that of a See-through. I had to realize that no matter what the strife, all life was connected. That was the secret to mastering my stamina.

I decided to play with the twins and empty my mind by running around on the shore. We made sand castles like the Castellians' castle and had swimming races. All the while, my mind and body were recovering from our adventures in Earth's Sea.

After we ate a bunch of random breakfast foods out of the fridge and fed Aion, I was fully healed. The bleeding from the dragon fight had stopped, and the wounds were mending. It was time to fight!

"So, I guess I'm fighting you first, Jade?" Zephyr rose.

"Yes," I confirmed, "and I'm looking at fighting from a whole new perspective." Out of the corner of my eye I saw Xaphias raise a brow.

"Well, here we go again. I've got some new tricks up my sleeve, Jadel. Let's see if you can take it," Zephyr taunted.

"I have new moves, too, Zephyr. Bring it on," I retorted.

I could feel the fiery blaze in-between us flare and spark. The intensity of our stalemate was five times hotter than lightning; ten times twenty-five times hotter than the surface of the sun! But I was determined to break that stalemate; I was determined to set the record straight from our battle almost a month ago.

Like Iris, I could see Zephyr's blue eyes shining with anticipation. The cool waves that smashed against the shore couldn't even begin to penetrate the fortress of heat between us. The intensity was so vivid, I could tell even the spectators felt it. Pupil and Iris were awestruck, Zenon seemed very uncomfortable, as did Aiondraes, while Xaphias just watched us with shrewd perseverance and crossed arms. His gold eyes were burning straight through the heat fortress, signaling the beginning of the battle.

I wanted to try something different to catch Zephyr off guard, so I started the battle with a full-fledge attack.

"Recatus!!" I screamed. First, I heard a muffled scream in the midst of the sonic boom given off by my attack, and then, the Recatus exploded in my face, causing a mass of smoke. I was aware of Zephyr charging through the smoke straight toward me, trying to use it as cover. It was just like my previous battle with Aiondraes! I had tried the Slow Motion Technique once before to counter this move, but that didn't work out so well. However, I suspected that Zephyr thought that I was going to try something different and wasn't expecting me to try it again. I'd use reverse psychology on her!

I went ahead with my plan and activated the Slow Motion Technique, and then I shot energy beams all around in a circle. When the smoke cleared, I saw that Zephyr was nowhere to be found.

I decided to fly up high to get a better look around the perimeter. A split second before she struck, I teleported behind Zephyr with the After-Image Technique. I thought I had her and prepared to attack in midair, but somehow, she used the After-Image on me! Caught off guard, she rammed her elbow into my back, and then followed up with a knee in my stomach. *Whoa! Double After- Image!*

"H-how do you know the After-Image Technique?" I asked.

"Duh, I copied it from you. It was easy! Plus, I learned that the After-Image can reflect attacks with other attacks that have the same amount of power. That's what I used to counter the Recatus," she explained.

"Whoa. I never would have thought of that. But I'll counter your wisdom with ingenuity. Energy force field!" I roared.

"W-what the—?" Zephyr cried out, and her smug expression disappeared. The trick I just thought of was that I encase myself in a sphere of protective energy that would burn with anything it came in contact with. It was very similar to that of the Zeal Orb's concept.

Catching Zephyr off guard, I rammed into her with the sphere of sizzling hot energy. I brought her down and smashed her into the ground. Then I condensed the energy focused around my body and repeatedly kicked her in the face.

"How do like that?" I bellowed. "I told you I'd counter—"

She applied the After-Image to escape her tomb and power punched my cheek from the side. I recovered quickly though, since she wasn't using her full power, and soon, we were in a martial arts fight. We both dished out punch after punch and countered kick after kick, but I had the upper hand. When was she going to use more of her max power?

"Why are you holding back? I'm wearing you down too easily," I complained.

"I thought I was wearing you down. I want you to be out of energy before I use my full strength," she replied.

"Don't take me lightly!" I roared, and then I hammered her to the ground with a barrage. I then deactivated my energy cloak calmly (that's what I'll call it) and got into my fighting stance, waiting for her to make the next move.

"Uhhh, you good, Jadel! If you want a fight, I'll give you all I've got!" Zephyr bellowed once she got up. Then I sensed a huge spike in her energy supply; she was at her peak.

"Now *that's* what I like to hear, Zephyr. Take your best shot!" I replied. And then I charged up my energy until I was at full power, too, minus the zeal.

Zephyr charged at me once again. This time I dodged her strike, and then forcefully rammed her in the stomach. Next, I karate chopped her shoulders, kicked back and forth in between her legs, and finally head-butted her.

"Arrrh! You haven't seen anything yet. Haahh!!" she screamed. She shoved her palm in the air toward me, and then an inexplicable force hurled me backward. I somehow landed on my head.

"W-what was-uhhh—" My sentence was interrupted by Zephyr ramming her foot into my chin.

I recovered quickly, swung around, and kicked her hard in the knee. Before I could fly up to recoup, she lethally elbowed my collarbone with bone-shattering force. I soon went flying back down to the ground.

"Ha-ha! Clear!" I screamed. I had got her right where I wanted her. I clapped my hands together, which emitted a sonic wave so fast that it had seared her arm and flung her backward. However, she did a double-back-handspring to cushion her fall and land on her feet, exhausted.

"You seem exhausted, Zephyr," I huffed. "Don't quit now," I taunted.

"Not a chance," she huffed back. "No way am I losing to a person I'm almost two months older than!" she raged. "Foveno Beam!!"

"Oh, man!" I exclaimed. I didn't know she was trying to finish the battle this early. I performed the After-Image and tried to get behind her, but she was already turned around and kicked me viciously in the throat. I fell, exasperated, to the ground.

"What, am I not worthy enough for you to use the zeal against me? Come on, I need to know how long I can stand up against it," Zephyr raged.

"No, I'm going to beat you with my own strength! I need to prove to myself that I can beat you without zeal!" I exclaimed.

"Then I'll just force you to use it!" Zephyr charged. "Future-sight and Double Foveno Beam!"

"Here comes the big one!" I bellowed, bracing myself. I didn't know what the first technique she bellowed did, just that she seemed to be using less energy by making two Foveno attacks with a mixture of the After-Image instead of doing it manually.

"Energy Force Field!" I roared. My attack completely absorbed Zephyr's and shot them right back at her. But suddenly, Zephyr appeared in front of me and blasted me with a close-up Foveno Beam. The aim and power was lethal. Was she trying to kill me?

I used the After-Image to recover and seemingly disappear before I fell to the ground.

"You can't hide, Jadel! Do you want to know what future-sight does? I can see where you are at all times *and* where you will appear in this battle!" Zephyr mocked. Then she attacked me with an energy blast that was right on target. Once again, I was knocked to the ground.

"Come on! You kept on boasting about how strong you had become, but look at you! You're as weak as I thought you were back in Xaphias! Will you be a wimp or show me the power of zeal?" Zephyr raged.

I was about to let it all out; I was about to show that I wasn't a wimp, but I couldn't. What good would going off the handle do if I was fighting my teammates? I had to use my powers when they were necessary, not to show off in sparring matches. I would win with my own power!

The struggle inside my head was so excruciatingly painful; it might have well been physical pain. And suddenly, I just exploded. I mean, I really went off the handle. I had exhausted every ounce of my energy in one final attack right at Zephyr, and the worst part, I couldn't stop it. I was helpless to even stop my own attack, so how was I supposed to stop one of the Eyerobis's? The thing I remembered was seeing Zephyr disappear and my body being lifted up into the sky.

I woke up without a scratch on my body, and we were moving forward on a forest trail. I was on top of Aiondraes.

"What happened?" I asked anyone who would listen.

"Oh, when you tried to kill Zephyr, Xaphias had to teleport her away and Aiondraes grabbed the back of your shirt and lifted you off before you lost consciousness," Iris explained.

"So, Jadel, that's your dilemma. You have all this power, but you refuse to bring it out. Zephyr got so frustrated with you, and that's what made her push you as hard as she did. She thought you were taking it easy on her," Zenon sympathized.

"But how could I use the zeal? It's not fair if—"

"It is fair. You may want to know the full extent of your power without the zeal, but the level you were fighting at before you blacked out was pretty much it. The max content of the zeal is your true power. You don't get it, Jadel; the zeal is a part of you. Since birth, it's been a part of you. You will never get any much stronger if you don't exhaust it," Xaphias explained.

"But . . . I—"

"Listen, J-J, the zeal is basically your form of soul energy. In other words, your soul is just made up of zeal! Your eyes are the window to your soul, so if you block out the zeal, you're just seeing blind," Pupil explained. That was the most valuable thing she's said in her whole life!

"Whoa, Pupil, did you just say that?" Zenon exclaimed.

"Yep. It's something Mom told me once in private. She said if you hide what makes you who you are, you're blindly walking on the wrong path, because your soul makes up who you are, Jadel," Pupil whispered.

"Yeah, plus, we don't want you to change," Iris conceded.

"Me neither," Zephyr huffed. I whipped around to see she was walking in front of Aiondraes. "Need someone to push me to do my best. And as opposite as we may be, that someone is you," Zephyr concluded.

"R-really?" I was very close to tears, which has never happened before in my entire life. I think I said something about that earlier. "D-d-d—"

"Whoa, there, Nelly! Stop, st-st-stuttering," Xaphias laughed.

"D-d-d-does th-this mean we-w-e're f-friends now?" I asked.

"Yeah, I guess so. Our love/hate relationship was bound to start sooner or later. We can't have any more verbal fighting in our team; it has to be all physical!" Zephyr joked. "I'm serious."

"You guys are the best," I sniffed. "How did we recover so fast, anyway?" I asked.

"Oh, that was my doing," Xaphias spoke up, "I fed you each a Healing Herb."

"Don't you think that would have come in handy before?" I said through gritted teeth.

"I didn't want to waste them. I need more for myself," Xaphias countered.

"Rrrr! Idiot, we could've been killed by the dragons, and I was so tired during our flight; you set us back three hours!!" I grabbed him by the collar and screamed in his face from Aiondraes's back.

"I-it's your fault for not remembering about the Healing Herbs in first place. If y-you asked me, then I wouldn't have said no," Xaphias said while trying desperately to keep his cool.

"Man, how selfish can you get!" I bellowed, and then started shaking him thoroughly.

"I saved you and Zephyr, remember? And I saved you in Celestine," Xaphias retorted. I blushed ferociously, and then let his face hit the ground.

"I hope you like eating dirt, hero," I teased, and stuck my tongue out for good measure.

"Wow, she showed you, Xaphias," Zenon laughed. "Come on, get up."

"Aughh . . . I hope you're ready to fight me soon!" Xaphias growled.

"Count on it. Next time, I'll be using my full strength," I retorted. A new chapter had begun in our quest as we walked deeper into the lush green forest of Full Moon Island.

Gravity Falls

AFTER I HOPPED off Aiondraes, our progress through the forest was much faster, and soon we were flying at high speeds again.

"Keep in mind, guys, this island is huge! It could be a month before we can get off it," Zenon warned. "After this, we'll be in a different county; the Laputa County."

"That's good. What's today's date?" I asked.

"July 19, 10110," she replied.

We kept walking until we found a quaint, dull town in the middle of the forest. It was located beside a mountain's edge, and there seemed to be no one around.

"Now this place is creepy," Xaphias whispered, but he seemed unfazed, almost excited.

"This place has an eerie feeling to it. What's it called?" I turned to Zenon.

"It's called 'Gravity Falls.' The only information about it says that it had a huge waterfall that floats upward instead of down! Now I'd like to see that!" she beamed.

"You would? Really?" an old, raspy voice questioned. Iris's eyes turned orange with fear.

"Uhhh . . ." I replied.

"Aioyyy!" Aiondraes screeched.

"Calm down, Dragon! Long time no see you guys!" a familiar voice giggled. It was Celestine.

"C-Celestine, what're you doing here?" Iris asked, flabbergasted.

"This is my grandma; I just came for a visit," she replied simply. I could see the resemblance; the white hair, but that could have just been from old age.

"Yes, Gravity Falls is haunted," Grandma Celestine whispered.

"Hmmm, I'm not sure I'm going to like this chapter . . ." Zephyr twitched.

"Tell us about the history of Gravity Falls, then," Zenon prompted, intrigued.

"All right, then. During the war that was fought thousands of years ago, the actual waterfall was used as a base. It was used as a hiding place to shelter the sick and wounded for the See-through side. But eventually the Eyerobis found it out. From high ground, one of them, whose name is unknown, used a special technique that reversed the flow of the waterfall. When See-throughian troops tried to come out of the cove behind the waterfall, they were carried up the current against their will and were obliterated. Some say that the souls of the dead warriors of those times are linked into Gravity Falls! It seems that this whole forest is crawling with ghostly and mystical Being s!" G.C. screamed.

"Grandma, they're just going to think you're a crazy old bat, which isn't far from the truth. But take it from me; I've seen all kinds of Beings here: elves, unicorns, magic eyeballs, you name it," Celestine added.

"Hey, that gives me an idea! If we can re-reverse the flow of the waterfall, then maybe the spirits will go away and the Beings that have been possessed by them." I had an epiphany.

"Why should we get involved?" Zephyr scowled.

"Miniquests like this that have no relevance to the plot of the story are required. I want to be on this quest for a longer time," I explained.

"Well, it's not about you, or us; it's about the fate of the planet," Zephyr retorted.

"Don't tell me you don't want to fight some unicorns."

"I do, don't get me wrong, but it's not our place to decide the fate—"

"Yes, it is. Our parents put the fate of Jupiter in the hands of its adolescence, and I have a feeling that if we solve this mystery, we'll get to our destination a lot faster," I explained with a glint in my eye.

"Aiiii!" added Aiondraes.

"Yeah, it could be fun, Zephyr!" Pupil encouraged.

"Whatever, buddy," Zephyr gave in.

"So, what's in that big head of yours, Jadeleve?" Celestine pondered.

"All we have to do is reverse the polarity, and we can create a hole through space/time to the other side of the cove!" I exclaimed.

"That made zero sense. How about we keep going north, through the town, and then woods, until we reach the waterfall? Then you just ride up the waterfall, get to the top of the mountain, and continue your quest?" G.C. suggested.

"What about the mystery of Gravity Falls?" I complained.

"Sweetie, the falls don't bother us at all. This town is peaceful if we don't bother the forest Beings, but through the forest is the quickest way through this town, so through the forest is where you must go. I mean, I don't know what the big deal is. I was just telling you some history. Celestine was just about to depart as well, so I'll escort you all over the falls," G.C. concluded.

"Wow, thanks so much, but it would be better if we went by ourselves," I declined.

"Wow, dissed in my own town! Well, see you around, Celestine." Then G.C. turned to go back home.

"Okay, bye, Grandma!" Celestine waved, and then adjusted her pack in preparation to leave.

"Celestine, where are you going?" Xaphias spoke for the first time.

"If you must know, my father has called me and my brother back home for a family meeting. Diamond is traveling around, too. I'm just going to their official base, near the See-through core," she replied simply.

"That far away?" I huffed, exasperated.

"You have a brother?" asked Zephyr.

"Can you fight?" Pupil asked curiously. Iris was just staring blankly overhead, and Aiondraes was doing the same.

"It's not that far, yes, and yes. Diamond is twelve and a half. Anyway, are you coming, or not?" Celestine prompted. Soon, the eight of us were trudging toward the forest.

The forest was full of wilted plants and fog, and it gave that ghostly impression that made you want to scream! It was dark and drab and—I couldn't wait to fight some ghosts!

One time, Aiondraes yelped, and I saw what he was

afraid of. Through the fog was the shadow of a unicorn, and from its horn shot out a rainbow-colored wave of energy. However, it was Celestine that deflected the attack with a blue-colored one of her own.

"Just try to ignore them; I don't have time to train here. I have things to do, so if you want to stop and fight them, I won't stop you," Celestine said without stopping to look back.

"Yeah, we'll fight them later, after we've obtained the Zeal Orb," I declared.

"Great. We're here!" she exclaimed. We were indeed located in front of a river that led up to a mighty, backward waterfall. As we exited the forest, the fog cleared, and I felt the cool night air on my face again. One of the moons was shining over the top of the falls.

"Let's just fly over," Zenon suggested.

"No, taking the waterfall will be more fun," Pupil explained. Even Iris nodded; chances were, we wouldn't be back here for a long time.

Unexpectedly, Aiondraes flew over to the river where the waterfall dumped its water and bashed right into the falls. The current upward was much faster than I expected, because we was making no effort to swim, and he was moving up at about 50 mph!

"We're coming," I assured him, but before I could rush up to meet my dragon friend, I was attacked from behind and flailed forward.

"We're under attack by spirit-born Beings!" Celestine squealed.

I turned around to see hundreds of unicorns, elves, fairies, and even Pegasus all gathered around us.

"H-how were these creatures made again?" I asked.

"They're just regular Beings except that we have names for them. That whole thing about the spirits of the dead affecting them is truly a myth. It's just a coincidence that creatures that were supposed to be nonexistent on Earth in olden times exist here," Celestine explained.

"I guess that makes sense. Whoa, just how many types of animal species were there back in the day?" I pondered.

"Remember when I said I wouldn't like this chapter? I take it back! Let's weaken their attack force and bail," Zephyr explained the game plan.

It was settled: The eight of us engaged in battle with past "mystical creatures." This time, I just attacked with long-range attacks. I practiced tapping into the zeal's—I mean, my, full power. I had to remember it was a part of me and I could use it freely. I must've taken as much damage as I delivered. Elves bit me, unicorns trampled me, fairies and pixies weren't really a problem, though. And . . . It seemed like only Xaphias, Zephyr, Zenon, and I were doing any work. In fact, I didn't even see Pupil, Iris, or Celestine help out once, and Aiondraes had run off again.

Soon, I decided it was time to stop playing around, and I released my full power. I could take out dozens of Beings with my energy force field and hundreds with one full-powered Recatus. For when I was attacked from behind, I used the After-Image to teleport to safety. I also used the Slow Motion Technique to get certain opponents right where I wanted them. It was even better training than I thought.

Xaphias was the one to have the last move, though. With

a great display of power (probably to show off to the absentee Celestine), he jumped up and rammed his fist hard into the ground, which caused an earthquake to ripple through the ground. It swallowed a very large portion of the Beings left standing and scared the rest of them off. The deed was done. Immediately, I turned around on Celestine.

"How come you—" I stopped midsentence. Neither she, the twins, nor Aiondraes were anywhere to be found.

"Uhhh . . . ummm . . ." I whipped my head around in all directions.

"It's okay, Jade! We're all up here!" Iris called. She and Pupil, for some reason, were on Aiondraes's back while he was flapping his wings to hover. Celestine was adjusting her pack and trying to get warm behind them on top of the mountain beside the falls. For some reason, the twins weren't wet like her.

"Okay, let's go!" Zephyr charged.

Before I could recover from my shock, she flew right into the upside-down waterfall and was carried up. I waited for everyone else to go before I went; I had some unfinished business.

Right after Xaphias and Zephyr were carried safely up, I did the same. But before I reached the top, I used the After-Image. Yes, I figured out that the After-Image is about splitting molecules in half. It breaks down the cells of your body to the size of atoms and gives the impression that there are two of you. It's all about separation. That's how I figured out how to turn the falls around, or at least I'd give a try. I would separate the Anti-gravity Technique from the waterfall.

"Jadel!" It was Xaphias. Somehow he plucked me out of

the falls and carried me to the top of the mountain with flight.

"I know what you're thinking," he said before placing me down. "Gravity Falls was never meant to be reversed. It's history; that's how it got its name. Why would you change the flow of the falls?"

"To go down in history, of course," I replied.

"You shouldn't think like that all the time, then you'll get self-centered like Celestine," Xaphias whispered.

"I heard that!" Celestine raged.

"Anyway, if the falls were meant to change, someone would have done that already. What's meant to change is the situation of this war. Come on, our adventures on Full Moon Island have just begun. My master lives here," Xaphias prompted.

"I guess you're right. I shouldn't think everything that's undone was left purposely to be fixed by me."

"That's an interesting way to look at it," Zephyr commented.

"Come, Aiondraes, fly northwest," Pupil prompted.

"Aioyy!" he screeched into the night. Aiondraes obeyed and took off again toward the other side of the falls. Xaphias followed suit without another word.

"Can you fly, Celeste?" I asked.

"Yes, of course! And don't call me that," she replied, and took off as well.

I, for one, looked back thoughtfully at the quiet, moonlight-bathed figure of Gravity Falls before I flew after them with Zenon and Zephyr following close behind.

The Triangle of Celestine, Jadeleve, and Xaphias

"RISE AND SHINE, guys! Our next destination is on Crossway Sixty which goes by Alamos town. That's northwest from here. It's perfect! We can meet Dracon, drop off Celestine, and keep traveling west," Zenon explained.

"Right," Zephyr yawned.

"Oh yeah. By the way, I want to battle you and Xaphias, Celestine, before you go," I said.

"Okay, I'll fight you first, then," Xaphias sighed.

"Wait, I didn't agree to get my hands dirty with you," Celestine scowled.

"How are you going to get stronger if you don't battle?" I asked.

"I only battle for self-defense. I was trained in the art of self-defense. Why would I have to fight if there's no threat?" she spat.

"I'm the threat. You'll lose all your skills if you don't practice. Come on, you get to beat me up," I pointed out.

"Hmmm, except I don't hate you, and I don't want to beat you up. I have no motivation," she whispered.

"Okay, I can work with this. Xaphias, are you okay with just fighting whoever wins the battle between Celestine and me?" I asked.

"Sure," he replied.

"Great! Okay, the winner of this fight will get to fight Xaphias, and then go out on a date with him," I declared.

"What!" both Celestine and Xaphias shouted.

"I said I needed motivation, Jadeleve! I need something I can look forward to," Celestine tried to calmly reexplain.

"Yes, your motivation is that you get to go out with Xaphias," I said.

"But you don't understand! I don't like him anymore!" she whispered.

"Anymore?" I raised a brow.

"Okay, I'll fight you if you save me the embarrassment," she sulked.

"Deal! Blackmail; yeah!" I cheered.

"What are you thinking, Jadel? Do you really like Xaphias that much?" Zephyr laughed.

"Would you keep your mouth shut? How am I supposed to fight him if that idea is floating around? Anyway, we've come to an agreement that I can't tell you about . . ." I tried to whisper. But I looked over and saw both Celestine and Xaphias blushing intensely and looking away from each other.

"Sorry I'm putting you through this, but I've been waiting too long to battle both of you! It must be done! Twins, clean up camp; we're moving to an open area," I declared.

It took about an hour to reach a place I'd fantasized we'd reach in thirty seconds. It was a large open grassland, perfect for a battle. But first, Celestine brought out her tent from a compactor. She went inside, and then changed into something she could actually fight in. She was wearing a white shirt, white shorts, and white sneakers. The color scheme reminded me of my tenth birthday present from Grandma Bachi.

"Are you ready?" she asked.

"Yes, I've been ready and waiting," I replied. Aiondraes screeched, which was the cue for the battle to start and for the other five to step back.

Celestine started off the battle by targeting me with a series of white-shaped beams which I did my best to dodge. But while I was concentrating on her attacks, she got behind me and delivered a dangerous kick to my shoulder. When I tried to recover, she wrapped her legs around my neck and flipped me over. I lay there in the dirt for a while, trying to remember how my body reacted to pain. Mercilessly, she started pounding me harder into the ground with relentless punches and kicks. I barely had time to breathe. I was done playing around.

Before she could barrage me again, I caught her fist in mine. Then I yanked her down, which took her leverage, and barraged her face with my own set of relentless attacks. I finished the combo with two consecutive strikes to her shoulders, which probably dislocated them.

"Y-you're much better than I thought, Jadel, but I still got something up my sleeve," Celestine smirked.

"Let's see it!" I shouted. I then attempted to elbow her cheek, but she used the After-Image to dodge. Instinctively, I used the Slow Motion Technique so I could see her movements and spotted her. Fiercely, I punched her down again. When she tried to get up, I thought I could kick her back down, but she wasn't having it. We were then locked in physical punches, trading blows left and right; it was awesome! But I knew that I had more than her, so I decided to start wrapping things up.

I tripped with a leg sweep and tried to blast her away to end the fight, but just before she hit the ground, she teleported behind me and elbowed the back of my head. However, I briefly tapped into my stored power and recovered with two roundhouse kicks to her stomach.

"I won't lose to a ten year old!" Celestine stormed. "Ice Twister Attack!"

I was suddenly engulfed in a twister that threw hailstones at me left and right which carried me up into the sky. In my shocked state, Celestine zapped me with the same white attack. It felt like being struck by lightning (which has happened to me many times). I shot down from the sky. I was falling fast. I expected a safe landing and decided to use the time being to rest, only Celestine wasn't going to let that happen. She hit with the same attack again, just before I hit the ground, which created a huge smoke cloud.

The final play, I thought. I decided to use the smoke as cover.

"Recatus!" I shouted at the same time I used the After-Image. This made it so it split the power of my attack in half, but it tricked Celestine all the same. The first attack was a decoy, which I forced her to dodge. Then I teleported behind her and hit her with the other half of my attack, which was just enough, anticlimactically, to end the fight.

"Not bad, Jadeleve," Celestine complemented after she recovered. "You've earned my respect."

"Thanks, Celestine, now it's your turn, Xaphias!" I bellowed.

"Whoa, don't get ahead of yourself, there. There's no way you can beat me; I've been holding back my power all this time so I could surprise you now," he smirked.

"Oh really? Now that's exciting . . . By the way, I need a Healing Herb," I demanded.

"Sure," he said before he reached into his pocket, took out the leather pouch, and threw to me what looked like a green bean. Right after I swallowed it, my strength was fully replenished.

I looked up and examined him—his eyes, his features, and his fighting stance. His sunset-gold eyes were unreadable, his face held no expression, but his stance held fearlessness. His thick black hair was repeatedly tousled by the wind in an intimidating fashion. It was time to see what he was made of.

"Let's begin!" he shouted. Unexpectedly, he made the first move.

He flew toward me at speeds I couldn't even see and ran circles around me. He quickly decapitated me, and then pulled my hair. The pain was almost unbearable (who knew?). Before I could reel from the pain, he dropped-kicked my head. He was relentless, like a beast, and kept kicking me in the face, but I couldn't get a good hit on him.

Finally, I decided that I was done with this game, so I charged my energy until I was at full strength. Green energy started to swirl around me as my body started to lift. I wanted an aerial battle.

"Are you ready? I've never used my full power in battle before, but it seems I need to now. I'm going to give it all I got!" I roared.

"It will be a challenge, but I will never lose!" Xaphias followed my example. I saw that my friends were captivated by what they thought was a stalemate, but one of us had to be stronger.

We flew toward each other at even speeds and started to trade blow for blow. It must've been going on like that for hours! Neither of us was going to give in, and it was just a sheer battle of wills. But Xaphias started to get more elusive and was evading all of my attacks. Only did I realize too late that I was running out of energy faster and wasn't paying much attention to the fight. This was the turning point; this was when the battle started getting good; after warm-ups.

When he tried to strike, I used the After-Image to get behind him, but when I attacked, he used the After-Image and got behind me! That must have happened at least five times before I finally kicked him in the stomach. He recovered in almost an instant and tried to attack again, but I surprised him by using the after-mage once more. He must've thought that I'd go behind him, so he turned around, but it was a trick; I used it and stayed right in front of him. I was aiming to win the fight when I tried to barrage him, but he countered with a clutch move: he got around me by splitting into three After-Images. Two were meant to confuse me, and the real Xaphias elbowed my forehead with devastating force.

When I panicked and tried to use the slowdown technique, just before, he disappeared. After the elapsed time passed, he reappeared in front of me and doubled kicked my left side. I trembled, and then let myself float safely to the ground, and he followed suit.

I thought that he thought we were taking a break so he could explain what just happened, but he caught my fist when I tried to take advantage of the opportunity, and he wouldn't let go.

"I have the power to copy most of the techniques I've seen. You know Zenon's Conjunctiva Expansion technique? Well, it isn't new. It doesn't matter who the person is; it just matters their capabilities. I could learn the Recatus if I wanted to. It's just that I've developed a technique that makes new techniques easier to perfect. But now that you know, I'm using all the tricks in my arsenal," he declared, and then let me go.

"You're on!" I retorted, and so round two had just begun.

He got up in the air again, but not as high as before, concentrated energy into his palms, and released. The beam was bright blue, and it was coming right at me. This time, when I created a force field, I added spherical movements to give it extra juice. Xaphias's attack bounced right off and was sent straight back to him, which he dodged using a ten-way After-Image. It looked like he had made clones of himself. But inside my force field, I attacked while spinning, and blasted through all of them. By the time I realized what was going on and stopped spinning, it was too late.

Xaphias appeared above my force field and pounded on it the same way he did to the Beings yesterday. The force of the blow opened my defense and exhausted me. Then he repeated the move on my head, and I was slammed into the ground, through the grass.

"Ugh," I couldn't catch my breath.

"It's time for the final attack, then," Xaphias warned.

"Not today! Recatus!" I roared. I'd put every last ounce of energy I had left into it.

"Recatus!" he copied. Then two purple beams clashed in midair and were both trying to push the other aside. I took the opportunity to try to teleport behind Xaphias, but he wasn't there. I looked around to see that he was behind me, but before I could react, he delivered a devastating blow to the back of my head. I then fell in a stunned heap on the ground. The two Recatus were completely even, and so they exploded against each other. The battle was over, and I had lost.

The Crossways of Destiny

WE HAD BEEN making great progress through the Land of See-throughs for weeks now after the fight between Xaphias and me. It took me awhile to recover even after Xaphias had given me a Healing Herb. Defeat had silenced me. It made me less cocky; it made me wiser, stronger, smarter, and faster. On this quest you couldn't sulk for long because you had to keep moving forward. Xaphias had taught me that no matter how strong you are, there is always someone stronger; there's always more left to achieve. To become the greatest fighter would be a long and difficult road, but I was up for the challenge.

July 30th was the day that we reached the end of Crossway Sixty. Here, we had to drop off Celestine, who was going west, and Xaphias, who was going east. The end of Crossway Sixty went right by Alamos town where Celestine was taking a submarine train to Coreicean Island; the home place of the See-throughs' Core. That's where the Castellian family's home base was. She was needed there.

"I'm going a little to the east. Well, first of all, I need to go into town to get material to make a sword, and then I'm going east. I need to assemble a team of young warriors to go with me on my miniquest to the Land of Eyebots. I need to infiltrate and get the inside scoop of the war," Xaphias reminded us about the game plan.

"Right; my dad and mom called home so we could discuss the future of Jupiter. I think we're going to have a meeting with some humans and Eyerobis to try to negotiate the war, but I don't think it will work. Anyway, I'll tell my family about your plan; now that we're friends, I support you guys all the way!" Celestine gave a thumbs-up, which was rare for her.

"Thanks so much, Celestine! Group hug!" I laughed.

Everyone, even Aiondraes and Xaphias (Xaphias was kind of forced into it) joined in a group hug. It was an emotional time, because besides Aiondraes, we were going back to the Original Five.

"Wait," Zephyr paused after we all pulled away from the hug. "Aiondraes, do you want to go with Xaphias? You can't grow big and strong by hanging around with us girls."

"Aioyy . . ." Aiondraes seemed confused.

"Nah. As much as I would like to have him along, it wouldn't be safe. I know full well that he can handle himself on his own, but I need to travel lightly; I don't want to be ambushed and have to worry about him," Xaphias seemed unsure.

"Are you sure? He could be a big asset to your team, and he's much faster and smarter than you think," Celestine added.

"Hmmm. What do you say, Aiondraes? Are you up for the challenge of being my companion? We'll be in twice as many dangerous situations if you come along," Xaphias warned.

"Aionyy!!" Aiondraes roared in reply, and then nodded firmly. His eyes blazed with fiery intensity.

"I'm glad for you, but we'll miss you," Iris cried. Then she buried her face on Aiondraes's back.

"It's better this way. That way, our team is spaced out and we have more troops," Pupil pointed out. It was another one of her golden moments.

"That's a very good point, Pupil. So, I guess it's settled, then," Zenon confirmed, and then turned back to Xaphias and Celestine.

"I'll take good care of him! Anyway, I think our paths will cross again, very soon," Xaphias winked.

"What makes you say that?" I asked.

"I suspect the Eyerobis are close by in the east. If we can't defeat them, which we probably can't, Dracon will inform you as soon as he can; he can sense life forms better than anybody I've ever known. You are going to Master Dracon's place in the northwest, aren't you?"

"Yes," Zephyr replied.

"Great; that's a much-needed pit stop. I guess there's nothing left to say, then," he added.

"Right, take care," I beamed, and then embraced him in a hug. Everyone else joined in to make it seem less awkward, even Celestine.

"I'll be training hard, Jadeleve, so don't think you can surpass easily!" Xaphias declared.

"Ah, just like old times," I sighed.

"Bye, Zeph, Zeezy, Puppy, Issy! Good-bye, Celestine; I'll

probably visit in a year or two if Jupiter is still here then," Xaphias smiled.

"Bye, sugar pie!" Celestine smiled, and then hugged him one last time. "See you later, you guys!" she waved.

"Bye, Celestine!" I called first before everyone else joined in and we saw her race into the west side of Alamos town.

"I'm going this way; take care," Xaphias confirmed and started walking toward the right with Aiondraes trailing behind.

"Take care, Xaphias!" Zephyr and Zenon cried in unison like they rehearsed it. It must've embarrassed him because Xaphias quickly ran deeper into town until he was out of sight.

"Onward to Master Dracon's place!" Iris cheered.

"It's not the end of the chapter, yet, Iris," Zenon sighed.

"Where is Dracon's house, anyway?" Pupil asked.

"That's weird; it's on the map! He must be more famous than I thought. It says that he lives by a place called Ionize town, right of Crossway Sixty-two." Zenon held up the holographic map for all of us to see.

"Great, let's—"

"No! I get to finish up, Jadeleve. You always finish. Let's go; onward to Ionize town!" Iris beamed.

I guess it was fair that she finish up the chapter this time, I thought. Anyway, we were back with the Original Five, and I couldn't have been more excited.

Enter: Dracon, of Paradise Falls

AT THE END of our two-day training session, I felt overpowered. I felt exuberant, energetic, and full of life! I was full of power waiting to explode; but I also had something else. I had self-control. I was wise and knew my own limitations. I once said they were imaginary, but what I mean is that I know my current limitations. Not only that, I was more in tune with my spiritual and mental side, and I no longer made reckless mistakes unless it was absolutely necessary. I was ready to find Master Dracon.

At around 2 P.M. on August 8th, we had reached Crossway Sixty-two which was aligned with Ionize town.

Ionize town was huge, but not as big as Celestine City. All its buildings were spaced out randomly with hovercrafts over the streets and people engaged in their everyday routine. It was by a north shore which went along by the Celestial Ocean, Ionize town's most famous tourist attraction. The Celestial Ocean was adjacent to the official entrance to Laputa County. Unfortunately, the beach was heavily guarded with Imperial Knights to keep people from traveling. It would seem that Celestine didn't clear things up with her parents yet, but I wasn't about to hold anything against her. After we were done with business, we would have to get our hands dirty.

"It says that Dracon's place, which is in Paradise Falls, is about forty miles west of here. Let's fly!" Zenon declared.

"Wait, can't we check out the town first?" Pupil complained.

"Work now and fun later. Plus, we need more energy, and Dracon's herbs will fully replenish us," Zephyr explained. She was right.

"I guess so," Pupil sulked, but she almost immediately jerked back up. And so, we set off west, flying high over a forest for what seemed like an eternity, even with our new speed.

Clouds were starting to move in overhead, just like they did on my tenth birthday. Lightning started to ripple through the gray air, accompanied by quiet thunder. Somehow I knew we were closing in on our first real enemy battle.

We had finally reached Paradise Falls eight minutes later. It was basically wide grassy plains with large hills around the sides. From above, the whole field looked like an oval. However, the three majestic-looking waterfalls behind a huge marble temple caught my eye. It would seem that this grassland was atop a cliff that was parallel to the cliff face the waterfalls were flowing off of. Basically, there was a trench between this place and the three powerful waterfalls, and the water was being poured put into the Celestial Ocean. We could leave the Celestine County from here after our business was finished.

"Hmmm, that temple seems suspicious," Iris speculated.

"It must be Dracon's palace; come on," Zenon prompted.

The five of us hovered down to ground, and then charged forward toward the entrance to the temple.

Let's see . . . the palace was the shiny tan color of marble. It was about one hundred and five feet tall and one hundred meters wide. I didn't know how one person alone could need that much space, but Dracon was a dragon. Maybe he was fifty feet tall!

"Hey, guys. Maybe we shouldn't bother him. What if Xaphias had it all wrong, and Dracon is actually a man-eating snake?" I yelped.

"Wow, Jadel; after all we've been through. We didn't come this far to turn back," Zephyr spat, and I immediately regained my cool. She was right; I had no reason whatsoever to be afraid.

It was I who pushed down the palace door, and I who led us into a dark cavern; at least I thought it was a cavern.

"Hello! Are you there, Master Dracon?" Pupil called while doing her best to imitate Xaphias's voice.

"He doesn't have to think we're actually Xaphias, Pupil. Xaphias himself said that Dracon could sense energy better than anyone, remember? He'll read our energy, and he'll know that we have pure intentions. We need the Sacred Water to gain extra power and help in the war," Zenon calmly explained.

See-throughs weren't yet advanced enough to see in the dark, so Pupil provided us with her flashlight eyes. I knew we were climbing up swirly stairs, but it seemed like we had been walking forever. Soon, we were floating up straight through the endless set of steps toward what seemed like light. All I knew was the next technique I was going to master was the x-ray vision technique, which Pupil herself had been working on these past few weeks.

It took us about ten minutes to slowly navigate through the temple. We assumed that Dracon was somewhere on the top floor. Why did everything have to be so conveniently faraway from us? Finally, I saw Pupil bump into a marble door.

"What the—? We're here!" she yelped.

"I'll do the honors," I suggested. I felt for the knob and slowly opened the door. It took us a millisecond for our eyes to adjust to the new light after being in the dark for some time; that was the way a See-through's eyes were built.

The room we looked around was gigantic with a marble floor, a marble ceiling, but huge glass windows. I mean, the whole room was about one hundred meters long and one hundred meters wide. It seemed to be one big fighting stadium, and at a far corner, my eye caught a red figure.

"Dr-Dracon?" Zephyr stuttered.

"Ah, so these are my guests. Xaphias messaged me through telepathy and told me that I would be having visitors soon; allies, come to earn the Sacred Water," he whispered through the shadows of the corner. He had a very low, resonating voice that echoed throughout the room. His skin seemed to glow red.

"Wh-what do you mean we have to earn it? Can't you just give us the Sacred Water? How are Xaphias and Aiondraes doing, by the way?" I bombarded him with questions.

"Why do you think it is called 'Sacred Water,' little girl? Only the purest of hearts are deemed worthy to drink it. To those who are not worthy and get their hands in it, the water is poisonous, and it will not escalate their power in any way. I deemed Xaphias worthy to drink it long ago, but he refused. He said that he would drink it when he turned twenty-one for reasons he still hasn't explained. However, I respect his judgment. I haven't seen him in a while; we usually communicate through telepathy when he's not here. The point is that after you engage me in battle, then I will decide if you are worthy of drinking the water," Dracon declared.

"I mean no disrespect, Dracon, but can you show yourself?" Zenon asked.

"Very well," Dracon replied. He stepped out of the shadows, and we saw that he was about fifteen feet tall with a tail that bore no spikes like Aiondraes's. His four-clawed fingers were sharp and well muscled, as were his scaly arms and legs. His wingspan was the most terrifying part about him since it was as wide as he was tall. He had two horns that were curved backward like a bull's and extrasharp teeth. His face was arrow-shaped like Aiondraes's or a basic reptile's. He appeared to be youthful and vibrant, but his eyes held years and years of knowledge; they were rainbow-colored. Anyone with rainbow irises had the ability to see into the future; an Immortal Seer. Iris herself was trying to figure out a way to show all her color signs at once so she could give off the illusion of being a seer, but Mom said it would take a couple years of practice.

"Whoa, you really are a dragon!" Zenon came to the conclusion.

"Yes. This arena is especially designed for fighting. Every time it's destroyed, I can press a button to make it as good as new again. So, who will go first? I will take turns fighting each one of you. Remember, you don't have to win; just show me your intentions. So who's first?"

Master Dracon vs. Iris

"I'LL GO FIRST!" Iris said boldly.

"Very well. What's your name, little girl?" Dracon asked.

"My name is Iris Dawn of the Land of See-throughs," she replied.

Why was she so hyper today? She was acting like Pupil.

"Ah, yes! Xaphias did mention that you were Silver's daughter; you're the spitting image of him! And so is this one," Dracon gestured toward Pupil.

"Yep. I'm Pupil Dawn, Iris Dawn's older twin," Pupil replied. I half expected her to act like Iris, but she was just acting like her regular self. I decided to wait until it was my turn to fight to introduce myself.

"You all might want to step back," Dracon prompted, and the four of us obeyed. He and Iris positioned themselves in the center of the arena. I felt the tension rise exponentially; the battle was about to start.

"Okay, let the battle begin!" Zephyr screamed since when was she a referee.

We all took cover on the sidelines of the battle space, watching them, when I asked, "Zenon, do you think she can win?"

"It's possible, but the goal isn't to win, remember? It's to see if we're worthy of the Sacred Water. Even if she does win, it doesn't guarantee she will get a drink," Zenon reminded me. We observed them in silence from then on. They took their battle stances like all experienced martial artists did before a serious battle.

Iris decided to charge at Dracon, but before she got right in front of him, she disappeared. I saw that she was trying to confuse him, but I knew that it wouldn't work; he had better sense then all of us combined. When Iris tried to come from behind and attack, Dracon was instantly turned around and delivered a savage blow to her neck.

"That's it; no more playing around! Rings of Fire!" she roared and sent four rings of molten hot energy right at Dracon. The key was that you had to focus energy at your eyes and give them enough rotation so that they catch on fire. But the craziest thing happened next: Dracon simply swallowed all the rings! He just sucked them into his mouth and swallowed the energy! Then he spewed his own flames at Iris, except his were so hot that they burned white! Luckily, Iris was able to teleport away, but that was what Dracon was prepared for. He met her with a series of fiercely powerful strikes from his tail on her face until it became bloody and bruised. Somehow, at one point, Iris was able to find the resolve in her body to block one of his strikes by grabbing his tail with her hands. By catching him off guard, she was able to swing him around and throw him straight down to the marble floor.

"Do not treat me like a fragile child! I can handle myself, so give me a fight that's not one-sided," she spat.

"As you wish, Iris," Dracon grinned, and got back in a stance. It seemed that he was not fazed by the fact that his barrage had barely fazed Iris, so I knew he must've had way more power than he was letting on. "Make sure to come at me with all that you've got!"

"It will be my pleasure. Very well, as you wish: that's what you sound like to me! Anyway, I've just figured out how to become a seer!!" Iris roared. Instantly, she was engulfed in a radiant, majestic rainbow aura. She was rainbow, her eyes were rainbow—everything was rainbow! Did she really have the power to defeat Master Dracon?

"My word! You have the Immortal Seer's color, but you're not purely a seer. The picking of a seer isn't all random; it has to do with your aligned birthright from your ancestors. Maybe your grandson will be a seer . . ." Dracon pondered.

"Enough talk! We have to find the Zeal Orb and stop the Eyerobis. Our next step is to acquire the Sacred Water so we can unlock more of our potential faster, so let's finish this!" Iris bellowed. And so the two rainbow eye-colored beings engaged in battle once more. They started switching attacks, trading blows, and dishing out strikes left and right. However, soon, Dracon started gaining the upper hand. Iris was becoming increasingly tired, and Dracon was able to start evading all of her blows. Dracon also started to get fancy and use combo attacks against her. He would attack her face consecutively with his claws, and then whip her down with his tail. It was brutal!

"Raaa!" Dracon roared when he spewed fire out toward Iris again. She was able to block most of the damage from the attack by using the energy field defense that I taught everyone how to do, even Celestine and Xaphias before they left. However, she was still pushed back, which made her vulnerable after the rotation of the spherical orb stopped. Luckily, the extra velocity left over from rotation caused her to spin around to face Dracon when he tried to teleport behind her and gave him a superpowerful kick to the jaw. However, Dracon, instantly recovered, grabbed her leg, slammed it against his knee, and then head-butted her. Before she could regroup, he savagely bombarded her skin with punches and kicks until she floated limply to the ground, her rainbow aura fading quickly.

"You definitely have the potential to be much stronger than your parents were when they were in their teens. This is an exhilarating match, but if you're in such a hurry, I'll have to end this soon," Dracon roared.

"Bri-bring it on . . ." Iris huffed.

Dracon charged and went for another punch which Iris successfully blocked. Then he fell back and spewed fire at her once more which she was just barely able to dodge. However, Dracon came from behind, using the fire like a decoy and drop-kicked her hard in the back.

"Ahhh!!" Iris started to scream with pain as he attacked her in vital spots again and again. But even through all that pain, Iris proudly let her eyes stay green. From the time she was young, I knew she changed the color of her eyes to express her emotions since she didn't talk much, and Mom, Pupil, and I had all figured out the code by the time she was three. She had always been the strong, silent type. And now she was slammed hard to the ground, struggling to stand up as Dracon was charging up the White-light Technique again.

"Arrr," Iris silently raged. Red energy started to swirl around her as Dracon fired his attack.

"Clear Out!!" he roared. The energy around Iris started to grow vaster and richer as she focused it all in her eyes.

"Corona Barrage!!!" she screamed at the top of her lungs. Huge halolike rings shot out from the energy collected in her eyes. The two nimbuses sliced through Dracon's beam and exploded in his face.

"Ah!!" It was Dracon's turn to howl in pain. But Iris was just getting started. With all the energy she had left she flew straight toward him while charging electrical energy at the base of her forehead.

"Thunder Bash!" she finally cried out, and then she head-butted Dracon hard in the stomach, a move similar to what I once did to Zephyr back in the day. Iris had probably developed the technique from watching Aiondraes using his lightning technique, though.

But the force wasn't nearly great enough to finish an Immortal Seer like Dracon off, and once he recovered enough, he swatted the battered form of Iris away with another elbow. She fell from about seven feet up in the air and slid slowly across the marble floor outside the line around the official arena space.

"I-I . . . uhhh . . ." she muttered. She should've just stayed down because in a battle like this you're required to keep attacking until your opponent was virtually unable to battle any longer. Then, anticlimactically, Dracon kicked Iris hard in the gut, in just the right spot, and she instantly lost consciousness.

"Iris!" Pupil came running to her twin sister's aid.

"That was the most interesting battle I've ever had!" Dracon exulted. "She showed me willpower that I didn't even know could be possessed. To take all those hits and still keep coming? Now *that's* something else! She has potential, like I said before, just waiting to burst open. She's definitely Sacred Water material. It would be a start to unraveling all the locked up energy. Would you feed her this Healing Herb?" Dracon said as he handed Pupil the pill so she could feed it to her knocked out sister. Pupil carefully slipped the herb into Iris's mouth, and with a gulp, she was awake and well.

"You passed the test, Iris!" Pupil exclaimed.

"I overheard, Pupil; I wasn't completely unconscious, but I do have a long way to go before I can be the best fighter that ever lived," Iris replied. My ears perked up at that last thing she said. "But I'm very grateful that you've accepted me, Dracon."

"Oh, please. I have no choice. You guys need the Sacred Water, and I just want to fight you all first to see if it won't be a waste. Now, who's next?" Master Dragon, I mean, Dracon, prompted.

"Hold your horses, M.D. Keep your socks on, Doctor, because *I'm* up next!" Pupil spat, determination fogging her eyes as Dracon took a stance.

It was only then that I realized that he hadn't taken a Healing Herb himself even after all that exertion by battling Iris. Did he really have that much power? Then I also realized that I must've been extremely underestimating him. He was Xaphias's teacher; he was our parents' teacher! Then I thought: *if he was so strong, why wasn't he helping in the war away on Saturn?* Finally, I came to a conclusion. Without there being a proven weakness against transflare, it was wiser to stay on Jupiter and experiment with different kinds of energy. What good would so much power do you if it was just going to be absorbed?

"My name is Pupil Dawn, and I'm your next challenger!" Pupil cried.

"Well, then, let the second battle begin!" Dracon roared.

Here we go again, I thought.

Master Dracon vs. Pupil

"TAKE THIS!!!" PUPIL fired her famous dazzling blue Sclera Blast to start the battle. But Dracon effortlessly dodged it.

"Right back at you!" he screamed before he spewed his famous white fire out of his mouth and straight at my sister. The raging flames were targeted right in the sweet spot: her stomach.

"Ahhhhhhh!!" Pupil screeched in agonizing pain from the scorching embers engulfing her body. She flew higher up in the air to try to brush off the flames, but Dracon was already on top of her and delivered a swift but powerful punch to her cheek. When she fell down from the force and made contact with the marble floor, she attempted to get back on her feet instantly. However, she didn't even get one second before Dracon was behind her and stroked her hard in the back with a kick. While she was flying sideways from the force, an idea formed in her head. She regained control and did a backflip to rise above the area where Dracon again appeared and dodged another fierce kick. Then she purposely fell above his head and kneed him as hard as she could.

"Ow!" Dracon cried and did a three-hundred-sixty-degree spin to shake the girl off his head. Pupil then landed in a spot a few feet away from him and charged again. Anticipating the wave of flames that blazed in front of her, she jumped up and dodged his attack. But Dracon was expecting that move and was already within range and slapped her away with his tail, the force of which was devastating. When the tail came in contact again with her, she was hurtled sideways and slammed into one of the four marble walls. When the dust cleared up from the tussle it exposed the battered form of Pupil.

"Take this; Clear Out!" Dracon fired his ultimate move at the girl with incredible force behind it. Pupil was able to fly up and successfully dodge, but this time, Dracon caught her off guard and punched her down into the beam's path, and it made full contact.

"Ahhhhh!!" she screamed as the beam swallowed her in a show of white light. She was caught in between a rock and a hard place. To top it off, Dracon's attack exploded and left a hole in the wall the size of a crater! I was about to go over and get another Healing Herb from Dracon to feed to Pupil, indicating that the battle was over. But when the smoke disappeared, it revealed a still-standing Pupil with so many injuries that you could never count them all.

She was standing right in front of the large hole in the wall that revealed the falls of Paradise Falls which reminded me of Gravity Falls. The most noticeable injury was on her arm which she was clutching; my guess was that it was broken.

"Ha-ha . . . If you think t-that is all it's going to take

beat me, then you are severely mistaken!" Pupil stuttered dramatically.

"I-I c-can't believe you're still standing. Your willpower transcends anything I've ever encountered, even your sister's! But let's see if you can take this!" Dracon emitted a ray of electrical energy right at Pupil from his hands. "I won't give up that easily."

Like she did once before, Pupil fired one beam of light from each of her pupils. They both became glazed, big, and dilated like before, too. Then the two yellow beams turned into blue electricity to match Dracon's attack. Pupil used this opening, ran across the marble floor with superspeed, and side kicked Dracon as hard as she could. But when she tried to punch him in the neck, he was able to grab it.

"You're very good, but . . ." Dracon whispered cryptically before he slashed her with his razor-sharp claws on her bad arm and followed up with a deadly tail whip to her cheek that sent her flying away. She bashed into the top left corner of the marble wall that was parallel to us and limply fell down against it.

"Pupil!" Iris cried out to her motionless sister with tears in her eyes.

"It's okay, Iris. The battle is over, and she doesn't have to get hit anymore," Dracon soothed, but he was wrong.

"W-wh-who s-said t-the ba-attle was over? I-I'm j-j-jus-st getting warmed-u-up . . ." Pupil coughed and tried to stand up, while also trying her best not to cough out blood.

"Pupil, stay still. You're just hurting yourself. You don't have to win this!" Dracon frantically cried.

"I-I-I . . . okay . . ." she stuttered, and then rested her head on the cold floor.

"She is definitely worthy of the Sacred Water. Anyone with that spirit and is able to cope as she has to keep their resolve inside must have a lot of self-discipline," Dracon explained.

"You just have to come up with a reason for all of us, don't you, Dracon?" Zephyr giggled.

"It's what I do. Iris, give your sister this herb," Dracon prompted. He tossed it over, and Iris plopped it into Pupil's mouth. It didn't even take her a second to wake up, fully recovered.

"You made the cut, Pupil, you can have the water," Dracon beamed.

"All right!" Pupil jumped in the air, looked happily at Iris, and then ran over to join us. Iris took more time to walk over to where the rest of us were.

"I'll go next!" Zenon stepped up. This time, Dracon ate an herb.

"Okay, then. What's your name?" Dracon asked.

"Zenon Zeal," she politely answered.

"So you're Xaphias's sister and Gold's daughter, then?"

"Yes."

"I thought there was a resemblance. This should be a good battle."

The two, like in all other battles, staged their stances. But each battle was different and required a different stance. It was the signal for Zenon to move forward and for us to move backward.

"Okay, let the battle commence!"

Master Dracon vs. Zenon

They charged at each other at the exact same time to start the brawl. They matched punch for punch, seemingly even in strength, but Dracon was just too strong for Zenon. Then he started to get serious and broke the stalemate by kicking Zenon hard in the stomach and teleporting behind her to deliver another fierce blow. However Zenon was sly enough to dodge another attack.

"Nice dodge, but let's see if—huh? Where'd you go?" Dracon looked up, about to attack his opponent who jumped up in the air above him, but she was nowhere to be seen.

"Over here!" Zenon's voice came from behind him, but it was too late to dodge. She already delivered a heavy punch to his back and sent him flying. When he regained his footing he asked, "How did you do that?"

"Well, since the conjunctiva is transparent, I expanded its shape and size and made it into an invisible cloak. No scientific logic, I know," Zenon replied.

I watched her in amazement, remembering how I once asked her a similar question.

"I see, but let's see how you deal with this!" Dracon locked onto Zenon's energy signal before firing his white flame wave at her. She used superspeed to dodge and jumped in the air, but Dracon anticipated that. With a bizarre double anticipation, Zenon already turned around and blocked Dracon's attempted attack from behind. Then Dracon, with incredible speed, slammed her with a devastating punch to the gut, grabbed her leg, swung her around, and let go so that she slammed down on the marble floor.

When the dust created from her contact with the floor cleared up, Zenon bellowed, "This fight is far from over; I have a few tricks left! Double Choroid Gun!" She focused the energy at her hands and fired two green beams in a sequence; firing one and letting it linger from her left hand purposely and shooting the second one from her right hand. She flew right behind gun 1, hidden from Dracon's sight because of the beam's light. He was successfully able to dodge gun 1 but didn't notice Zenon right behind it. She caught him by surprise, and then barraged the exposed form of Dracon with a series of punches and kicks to his stomach, cheek, and everything she could get her hands on. When Dracon finally was able to counterattack with a punch, Zenon flew out of the way at the last second, revealing to Dracon a second Choroid Gun which he had forgotten about. But before he could get engulfed by the blast, Dracon turned around and fired his signature move.

"Clear Out!!!" Zenon was too vulnerable, and the blast was too quick for her to dodge, so she took it on full force while Dracon was hit with the half-powered Choroid Gun. Recovering just a second earlier, Dracon burst out of the smoke from the blast and flew straight at Zenon, delivering a hard punch to her cheek. She plummeted to the ground again, but at the last second, she had disappeared. She slickly flew up and came from behind him again. Then surprisingly, she hit him with another Choroid Gun with the reserves of all the energy she had left.

"Ahhhhhhh!!" Dracon shrieked in pain as it was his turn to fall helplessly to the ground. Zenon started huffing, and I decided to tune into their energies. I sensed that both of their powers were low from exhaustion. Then as Dracon landed on the ground, he fired pathetically weak fire waves (probably due to his dropping energy level). He fired exactly three and noticed that Zenon was softly but uncontrollably floating down to face the fire. He guessed too that this phenomenon was occurring because of her fatigue. She got hit by all three blasts and started to fall more quickly.

"Sorry about this, Zenon, I have t-to end it!" Dracon raced at the falling girl, charging up for the finishing punch. Then, dramatically, Zenon opened her eyes and concentrated all her remaining energy in her legs.

"I'm not done just yet!" she hollered as she used the rest of her little energy to float for a second, successfully getting out of Dracon's hitting range. Then she delivered a fierce kick to the back of his head, knocking him down slightly. As he fell to the ground, Dracon used all his energy to swat her away with his tail before kneeling on the ground, coughing up blood. The force of the contact sent Zenon hurling upward, then she fell back down. She decided to stay down to avoid any more injury and save time, which was the smartest thing to do. Then Dracon fell to the ground as well in noticeable exhaustion.

"Whew! That was the best battle I've had in a while. Her battle technique is slick and sly. She too is worthy of the Sacred Water!" Dracon cheered through huffs of pain, taking out another out Healing Herb from his pouch where he kept it, much like Xaphias did. He threw it into his mouth and swallowed; I wondered how he could eat two of them consecutively and not be completely bloated, but, of course, it was his invention.

Then he reached inside again and tossed one over to Zephyr, who was walking over to Zenon.

"Nice job, sis, you did it!" Zephyr said before putting the herb into Zenon's mouth.

"T-thanks! I guess you're up, Zephyr," Zenon pointed to Dracon who was standing and waiting for the next battle. "Good luck," Zenon whispered in her sister's ear as they ran in opposite directions. Zenon was replacing Zephyr as a spectator while Zephyr was replacing Zenon as an opponent. Zephyr embraced Dracon.

"You look exactly like Zenon, so you're probably her twin sister. What is your name, though?" Dracon inquired like he asked all of us.

"My name is Zephyr Zeal," she replied calmly, not underestimating her adversary one bit.

"I bet this is going to be exciting!" Dracon respectfully complimented, getting in his stance.

"It will, for both of us. Just wait to see what I have in store for you!" Zephyr concluded the conversation, moving into her own position.

Master Dracon vs. Zephyr

"LET THE BATTLE Begin!" Dracon yelled as usual as the two lifted off the ground almost at the same time. Instead of the usual punch for punch icebreak, Zephyr did a front flip over Dracon to evade his first attack and landed behind him. Then she charged at him at full speed and struck with a hard elbow. Dracon recovered fast and tried to swing around to counterattack, but she dodged again with another front flip over his head.

Then, surprisingly, Dracon cried out, "Clear Out!!" He shot out a brilliant white light straight at her, and it made full contact. But before the smoke cleared up, Dracon flew up and delivered another heavy blow, punching her down hard to the ground. Zephyr skidded across the slippery marble floor for a second, and then jumped right back into action.

"Ha-ha! Let's see if you can handle this!" she taunted. She flew up and charged at him again. This time, when he tried to whip her away with his tail, she used the After-Image Technique to dodge. When she became visible again, she appeared right in front of Dracon and jump-kicked him in the jaw.

Dracon's head flipped back from the force, leaving his stomach exposed. Zephyr took advantage of the opening and struck him with a barrage of swift punches, leaving Dracon breathless with pain. However, he was not as battered as he was letting on. He caught Zephyr off guard in the middle of her relentless attack and smacked her with his tail. Then Dracon wrapped his tail around both of her wrists, immobilizing her, and delivered his own set of punches at her stomach. However, he stopped after she started to cough out blood from her mouth, but then he threw her gently on the marble floor. After some dust cleared up, he caught sight of the badly shaken form of Zephyr.

However, she was excited to have such a powerful opponent nonetheless. She stood up vividly with sparks of electricity and seeable golden energy swirling around her. Both hands possessed their own orbs of red-hot energy and I thought she was about to fire them separately, but she did something unexpected. She brought her hands together and fused the beams' energy and power in a clapping motion. Now, she was holding a lethal weapon in her hands.

He probably thought she was going to fire it like that, but she did something unexpected again. She flew up to Dracon and separated the beams' energy in each hand again, then yelled, "Take this; my new technique—power punch!" She delivered a blinding barrage of heavy blows to Dracon's cheeks and stomach, leaving red spots in their place. Then while Dracon was stunned, she flew behind him and connected the beams again, after screaming the words, "Connection cannon!!"

She fired the attack which made lethal contact with

Dracon. She tried to go through the smoke of her blast to attack again, but Dracon used all his strength to block the beam and recovered within seconds. He then delivered a fatal kick to the side of Zephyr's neck that sent her crashing to the ground.

"Ahhhhh!!!" she howled in pain through the smoke that clouded her vision, realizing the fierce kick also broke her right arm. Dracon followed her down and tripped her with a swift but hard leg sweep, breaking her left leg. He then picked her off the ground with his tail, threw her up in the air like a volleyball, and punched her hard away. She landed limp at the side of the same wall she had smashed into earlier and just lay there.

"Sorry about this, Zephyr, but this battle can't go on forever!" Dracon screamed before firing his rare electric wave to end the battle. Unexpectedly, Zephyr opened both eyes with a glazed pain-clouded gaze in each.

"I'm going to win!" Without the use of her leg Zephyr flew straight at the electricity and easily deflected it, guided by the power of will. Next, Dracon fired a weak flame wave, which was the result of his exhaustion, and this time, Zephyr actually flew straight through and took the damage. She just kept on coming!

"Take this!!" she screeched with a concluding tone. With her good arm, Zephyr punched Dracon hard in the chest and sent him staggering uncontrollably.

"Now for the finishing attack; a full-power Foveno Beam!" Zephyr fired her ultimate move straight at Dracon, making full contact again. While the smoke was still clearing up, Zephyr floated down to the floor in exhaustion, nearly fainting when she knelt on her broken knee and switched them. When the smoke from her blast finally cleared, it revealed an unconscious Dracon, battered and broken.

"Zephyr . . . You did it. I can't believe you actually beat Dracon! I guess my rival has to be really strong," I cheered.

"Thanks, Jadel . . ." Zephyr whispered. She limped on the ground until she reached where Dracon was lying, then reached into his pocket and took out one Healing Herb. Then, just after chewing and swallowing it, she was fully healed and ready to go. She reached down and got another herb, and then fed it to Dracon.

"Zephyr, you were amazing! You completely overwhelmed me! The only three things that match your power are your will, your love for battle, and your caring and respect for battle and life. You are worthy beyond words of the water. The only other person who has ever beaten me in battle was your brother two years ago!" Dracon complimented.

"Thank you!" Zephyr sang as she ran over to hug Pupil, Iris, and then Zenon. Then she turned and gave me a thoughtful and intense look.

"It's your turn, Jadel. Do your best and I know you can win; I know you're worthy! I mean, you managed to beat me once . . . twice . . . so you can definitely take him!" Zephyr encouraged.

"Thanks! I will!" I promised, gave her a quick hug, and then jumped over to meet Dracon.

"So your name is Jadel?" Dracon guessed.

"Yes, Jadeleve Dawn!" I answered.

"So you're Iris and Pupil's older sister? It can't be. You look nothing like—wait. I can see it now. You don't look like them according to eye color or hair color, but there is a great resemblance. I've got it; you're the spitting image of Ruby!" Dracon yelped.

"Yes. She is our mother, and Silver is our father," I replied.

"Those were some tough battles, and I hope you're as good a fighter as your father. Other then Xaphias, he's the only one I have lost to. Well, other than your mother, oh, and Zephyr . . . and, Gold, and Sapphire, and Emerald! God, I've lost to so many people in the past fifteen years," Dracon said to himself.

"Anyway, let's see if this will be a spectacular battle as well!" Dracon roared before getting in his stance. As we were getting ready for battle, my attention wandered to another subject; our parents. How were they doing in the war on Saturn? How could I ever connect with them? Then it hit me: my birthday present! All I had to do was turn on the transceiver, send messages into it, and hope it reached my dad. I would have to test it out after this!

"Let the fight begin!" I screamed, and that's when Dracon decided to break the ice.

Master Dracon vs. the Zeal Possessor

"Ow!" Dracon cried. The battle started out as a stalemate, but I tripped Dracon with a quick leg sweep. While he was vulnerable, I buried him beneath a series of fiercely powered attacks.

Then he decided to fight back by dodging my last punch and countering with a hard knee to my chin. I staggered back with pain, but I hardly felt remorse. I was terrified.

"A-are you . . . holding back?" I whispered.

"That is yet to be seen, young one. I am only testing you,"

Dracon forebodingly replied. Then it struck me: even if I did beat him, it wouldn't count, because he wasn't putting all his effort into it! *Well, I'll just have to draw more power out of him*, I thought.

This time, I leaped forward and kicked him hard on his shoulder. Driven by what seemed to be pain, he grabbed my leg and swung me away. Then he followed up and punched me square in the stomach. However, before he could continue with his assault, I pushed him away with a small powered energy beam. It allowed me to land safely on the slippery, marble surface with him a good distance away.

After I regained control, I flew straight toward him, used the After-Image to dishevel him, and did a flip over him so I could see from an aerial point of view. However, he managed to teleport behind me and elbowed me in the back. After the blow, my back curled inward and my stomach curled outward, so Dracon continued with his ferocious attack and rammed his knee right into my gut. But I was able to recover instantly, use the After-Image to get behind him, and kicked him at the back of his head.

Dracon then turned around and said, "You're really quite good. Now that I've tested your strength, I know now what I must do. When I was fighting everyone else, I wasn't exhibiting my full strength; I still had a couple tricks up my sleeve. Zephyr caught me off guard, just like everyone who's ever beaten me except Xaphias. I was going to use a technique that multiplies my attack and speed, but she was sly enough to get behind me, not literally, though. But I must warn you, even though my strength grows, my defenses weaken at my stomach and my back. I scatter my energy to my arms, fists, legs, and head, but there is no energy protecting my stomach and my back, so those spots are vulnerable. Let's see how you fair against energy dispersion!"

I witnessed glowing red energy focus and condense around the places he had just mentioned. And with the blink of an eye, he was already in front of me.

What I did next was kind of cruel: I used the Slow Motion Technique on him and exploited his weakness. I fired the Recatus right at his stomach with deadly accuracy. But I was never caught more off guard in my life! He recovered almost instantly. Somehow, I was able to block his first punch, but I was so stunned, and his movements were so fast that he broke through my defenses in mere seconds. He started bombarding me with a barrage of kicks, and then punched my cheek with so much force that it sent me crashing to the ground. My forehead was rammed into the incredibly hard surface of the marble floor.

I tried to get up quickly to act like the onslaught didn't faze me, but that was far from the truth, and he could see right through it. I started to wobble and before I could gain my footing, he already delivered a pain-stabbing blow to my leg. Broken, I couldn't move fast enough to dodge his hard kick to my cheek, the force of which sent me flying sideways. I regained some sort of control quickly and flew up even higher in the air so I could get a good look at him, but he had teleported behind me before I could do anything.

"Take this!!" He fired his flame wave from his mouth and scorched my back. Since the power of his long-range attacks weren't multiplied along with his strength and speed, it was almost bearable; I could take it. But it would seem that the white fire wasn't his real attack.

He then used his electric wave to temporarily paralyze me, so I could only fly around in the air, but if I fell to the ground, my body would be useless. My arms and legs were stuck in awkward positions, and I barely had control of my sky dancing.

Dracon took advantage of my predicament and punched me out of the sky, so my head hit the marble floor once more. Then he calmly hovered down to the floor to join me.

"Y-you're unbelievably s-strong! How did you manage to be beat by Zephyr again?" I stuttered in-between coughing out blood.

"Hey, I heard that!" Zephyr hollered.

"I told you, I wasn't quite using my full strength. But now I am, and I can't bear to see an ally suffer at my hands without a good reason. How about you give up, I give you a Healing Herb and a sip of the Sacred Water, and you can help save the planet?" Dracon suggested.

"No. Do not take me lightly. I'm sure if I have enough experience to say that that's always a mistake, but—I haven't proved my worth yet!" I exclaimed, trying to get up. "Gahh!!" The paralysis hadn't quite worn off yet.

"Jadeleve, don't do it. You're only hurting yourself!" Dracon winced.

"I-I will—" But before I could finish, Dracon was already stepping on my stomach.

"Maybe you're right, maybe you haven't proven your worth of the Sacred Water, and maybe you never will. What you're demonstrating isn't courage, however; it's stupidity! Stay down or the enemy will be forced to beat you down!

You need to know your limitations, do you understand? Stay down!" Dracon roared.

"I get where you're coming from, really, I do! Xaphias told me the same thing once; he probably learned it from you. But I know my own limitations, and I'm far from done. Giving in if you can help it is shameful, plus, resisting is fun. It's what I do!" I laughed through the pain.

"You really do have one of the purest hearts I've ever seen; it's equal to your mother and father's. But you need to learn discipline! Mercy does not exist in this war! If you spare your enemy, you're finished!" Dracon warned.

"That's where you're wrong! In this war, killing is just like adding insult to injury or pouring salt on a wound! Killing and dividing are what got us into this mess! After I'm done here I'll prove it! Even if showing mercy doesn't work, someone has to have the courage to try!" I retorted.

He started off kicking me hard in the back which catapulted me upward and knocked about half a pint of blood from my mouth. Then he elbowed me back down with much force, giving me no time to catch my breath. Finally, he grabbed my leg again and slammed me down on the marble floor again and again. I needed to find a way to get back in the air before the paralysis wore off. Then, suddenly, I had an epiphany right when he let me go. If I were to fire an energy blast under me, the force could be used to catapult me into the air, and I could fly up from there. I could use the Recatus technique, my strongest move.

"OK, here . . . Here it goes!!" I screamed before I released the concentrated energy blast from my hand, the force (proving that my hypothesis was correct) catapulting me about ten feet into the air. From there, I could fly regularly.

Dracon, having witnessed this strategy, yelled, "Very impressive! I would never have thought of that! But I have to end this!" Even though Dracon was flying at me at full speed, my mind was elsewhere. One of the only traits See-throughs inherited from the humans was pain recognition. Other than incredible eye-involved powers, the Eyerobis was a race that could remember pain on their skin quickly, so the next time they got hit in the same spot it wouldn't hurt as much. The humans followed this gene code too. Some skins remembered faster than others. The humans' genetic code didn't follow the pattern as well as the Eyerobis, but their genes in the mixture made us See-throughs more advanced in that factor. My mom told me about this once, and she also said that our specific family Dawn genetic code was famous for pain recognition, but I felt my skin didn't remember fast enough, and my feelings were confirmed when Dracon caught up to me and delivered a blow that hurt even more than before. The force (again) beat me down to the ground. I landed on my left arm, breaking it beyond repair. Lucky for me a Healing Herb would fix that up and more.

With my left arm and right leg broken I left like Zephyr, only I think for her it was her right arm and her left leg that were broken. Dracon came down with me, giving me no time to recover. He picked me up by the neck of my shirt and hurled me up in the air. Only I didn't have enough energy to keep flying and I fell back down, but luckily, the paralysis finally wore off while I was in midair.

"Clear Out!!!" Dracon yelled before he shot a beam of brilliant white light right at me, knowing I couldn't move to dodge it. I dramatically got swallowed up by its beauty. However, some of the force was blocked by something; something that I could now control at will. If I didn't use that something as a shield right then and there, I would have lost.

Barely conscious, I fell down to the marble below. I almost let consciousness slip away when I banged my head for what was at least the thirtieth time.

Dracon, thinking I was asleep, said, "I'm sorry that I had to be so harsh on you, Jadeleve. I'll give you a Healing Herb as quickly as I—," but I cut him off. He was in pure awe as he witnessed me getting up.

"Save the herbs for later. We're both going to need plenty . . ." I ominously whispered, hiding me eyes behind my golden hair. A vastly powerful, green energy field started to circle around my body. I started to elevate off the floor as slowly and dramatically as I could. I realized my broken leg and my arm were both healed; either that, or I was so wrapped up in the fight I forgot all about them. Right now, I would appear as a ten-year-old girl with golden hair and golden eyes to anybody. Now it was *my* turn to be ready to end this!

"Now I'll show why we can unite the Lands again! I'll show you that killing is never the answer! I'll show you the true power of zeal!!!" I raged.

Then I charged at him with blinding speed. It was too late for him to dodge, and I struck him right in his sweet spot, his unprotected stomach. Then I jumped back and focused my energy at my hands for the final strike. Quickly I started running back at him and ignoring the pain of my injuries while chanting, "Rec . . . a . . . tus!!!!"

I was able to dodge his last two futile attacks, jumped up

in his face, and fired! I released the brilliant purple light from my hands. A huge explosion shattered the silence before my energy started fading with the sunset. There was nothing I could do to keep my energy from dropping like a stone, and then I fell to the ground, unconscious.

The next thing I knew I was hearing voices chanting, "Jadel . . . Jadel" that I noticed belonged to Pupil and Iris.

"W-what happened? Did I win?" I asked, feeling fully healed and energized. I was guessing that they treated me to a Healing Herb. We were all seated on the cliff that was straight in front of the falls of Paradise Falls. With two of the three moons out and the stars shining, I didn't need light to see. The scene was actually quite captivating and disturbing all at once.

"You sure did, and Dracon has something to tell you!" Pupil laughed. She turned to reveal Dracon sitting by twins.

"You are most definitely worthy. I hadn't had more thrilling battles in my life than the ones I had today with you and all your friends. I've already let your friends drink the water, and their powers exceed mine and yours now. I'll let you drink it so you can catch up," Dracon vowed. He handed me a glass of Sacred Water, and so I dramatically gulped it down at once.

It tasted like regular water so, naturally, I had some doubts, but after a couple of seconds, my eyesight became glazed, which was very disorientating. I sensed my own energy, which was rising quickly, and then it slowed, like a growth spurt.

"What do you know, this stuff actually works! Thanks, Dracon!" I expressed my gratitude.

"You're welcome, but I have some bad news. Xaphias's and Aiondraes's energies are almost completely gone. It seems that they are in a fierce battle against two others, but Aiondraes was knocked out early. Xaphias has been protecting him with all he's got! You must hurry and defeat those Eyebots!" Dracon prompted.

"I have two questions first. Are these Eyebots famous? And where are they fighting?" I asked hastily.

"No, not really. These two, I've met them before. They're twins named Cocone and Rodney, and probably the two weakest of their kind. However, your parents are the same biological age as them, and they fought back in the day. Your parents were lucky to have escaped with their lives. Also, Cocone and Rodney are not 100 percent Eyerobi; they're half Eyerobi and half Beings. They look like dragons," Dracon explained.

"Are you half human and half Being, Dracon?" Pupil asked.

"No, I'm a dragon that can use telepathy and talk. After I became an Immortal Seer back in ancient times, I was given those abilities. However, those twins are monstrous and evil. They're part of the attack force the Eyerobis purposely left on Jupiter to stop people from infiltrating their Land of Eyerobis while they are on Saturn and to attack other Lands. They've been causing this entire ruckus across the Land of See-throughs for the past two months. You need to fly directly west from here, save Xaphias and Aiondraes, and finish them off," Dracon concluded.

"Aren't you going to help us?" I asked.

"No, I have some unfinished business to take care of;

probably I won't see you for another year. The real question is, are you ready to face your toughest opponents yet?" Dracon asked.

"Yeah, we've been training for the past two months just for a moment like this!" Zephyr assured.

"Look, I'll give you seven Healing Herbs straight from my gardens; make sure you give one to Aiondraes and Xaphias, okay?" Dracon requested.

"Right," I replied, and put the herbs into my pocket.

"At your level of speed, it should only take you one and a half more years until you reach your destination. Take care!" Dracon waved, and then he vanished.

"Uhhh . . . okay," Pupil replied.

"Come on, guys, Aiondraes and Xaphias need our help! We were the ones who put Aion in Xaphias's care," Iris pointed out, and she was right. Finally, the five of us, the Original Five, took off west.

Westward

"WESTWARD, HO!" PUPIL chanted. Being in front of the moon on cool nights was what always had soothed her, but it was the exact opposite for me. Like I said before, I hated the night; I was more of a morning person.

"We're almost there!" Zenon screamed after a while. She had to scream to be heard over the fierce winds that were blowing against our faces as we flew.

For some reason, I thought this battleground would be a lot closer. We'd been flying for three hours! After about another thirty minutes, I was about to ask Zenon about how much farther it was when Zephyr yelled, "They're down there!!"

We floated down to greet the severely injured Xaphias and Aiondraes, the dragon. Aiondraes looked like he'd grown.

"H-hey, you guys. I knew you'd come. Dracon s-sent you, right?" Xaphias stuttered. Aiondraes was whimpering silently behind him, trying to conceal his vast pain.

"Yes. We're here to heal you both and defeat the Eyebots; we've all been deemed worthy of drinking the water," I confirmed. I went over to him, bent down, and fed him one

Healing Herb. Immediately, he got up and stretched. Then I slid another herb down Aiondraes's mouth, who screeched with gratitude.

"I can tell, you're almost stronger than me now," he yawned.

"Almost?"

"After this, we're going to continue our quest for the Zeal Orb. With our new speed, we should be there in one and a half years," Zenon explained.

"That's good. I'm going to continue with my plan; I've decided to go east! I'm going directly to the Land of Eyebots. I figure I'll meet new people along the way, and Aiondraes has decided to stick with me," Xaphias smiled.

Iris looked up at Aiondraes. I think she was the most attached to him.

"Is that true, Aion?" she asked with puppy dog eyes, which was an effective technique.

"Aionyy!" Aiondraes nodded in reply.

"Well, then, be safe!" Iris smiled, and then wrapped her arms around his neck. It took her a couple of minutes to pull away.

"Be careful; I'm not sure where Cocone and Rodney are. If you're looking to put an end to their rampage, you should keep flying north until you sense something. They're probably fully recovered from when Aiondraes and I slowed them down. These will be the toughest Beings you will have fought yet, so keep your guard up!" Xaphias warned.

"Right!" we all chimed in. We took turns hugging him as a replacement of saying good-bye. I took the longest to pull away.

"Farewell, guys, and good luck. And Jadel, what do I always say? You better be careful, because I'm not slowing down my training regimen one bit!" he bellowed. As if it were rehearsed, Xaphias dramatically jumped in the air, preformed a triple backflip, and landed on top of Aiondraes's back before the two disappeared into the sky.

"Where do you think the Eyebots are?" Iris speculated after we had been flying north for about two more hours.

"Well, I'm sure with their speed, they went far, far aw—wait! I sense some energy coming from somewhere nearby!" Zephyr screamed. I soon could sense it too. It was almost like something was walking up nearby. They weren't aware of any enemies, but their guard was still up. That was the mark of a shrewd warrior.

"The energy is-is incredible!! There definitely are two of them," Zenon said.

"Yeah, and they're getting closer," Iris added. Finally, about fifteen minutes later, two stunned dragonlike creatures crept out of a nearby cave, one green, one blue. They were completely identical except for their color, with two horns on each of their heads. They had long scaly tails; they both had wings like Dracon's, too. Their dragon scales glinted in the moonlight. Not one of us was prepared for what they said next.

"The answer to your question, little one, is that we didn't travel very far at all," the green one said in a low, humanlike voice.

"In fact, we stayed here so we could kill you, but you didn't have to wake us up, unless you want to die. Who would ever think that revenge tasted so sweet?" the blue one followed.

I couldn't believe it. It was the very first time I was in the presence of an Eyerobi. It was the very first time that I doubted myself when I said I could unite the Lands again. However, I also knew that I would have to regain my confidence through my very first enemy battle.

Cocone and Rodney of the Land of Eyerobis

"YOU'RE-YOU'RE . . ." Iris stuttered.

"That's right; we're Eyebots. I'm Cocone, and this is my twin brother Rodney," the blue one replied. "We're here to protect the Land of Eyerobis by taking invaders out here. We have to slow down travelers, including anyone traveling with a Zeal Possessor."

"Argh! Didn't you get the memo? The royal family isn't working for you anymore!" Pupil roared.

"Oh, really? We didn't get that message. Fools, it's shameful to beg for forgiveness to anyone of another race. Those fools are blinded by fear, and we took advantage of them. I mean, of course, we won't spare them; we'll annihilate every one of you," Rodney casually added.

"You make me sick! You Eyebots don't have the strength to face us with your own power, and so you hide behind artificial power like transflare. You don't have to fight us; we can calm everybody down and unite the Lands if you'll just let us in!" Zephyr pleaded.

"Oh, please. The See-throughs have grown ever so cocky.

You need to learn respect, you need to learn that there's only room for one race on Jupiter!" Cocone spat.

"So you're saying it was a mistake that we were even born? *You* need to learn respect for life! All life is equal, and you don't have the right to throw any life away," Zenon wailed.

"Sure we do," Cocone and Rodney whispered in disturbing unison.

"If it's a fight you want, then it's a fight you'll get!! I'll show everyone who has ever doubted me that showing mercy is harder than killing someone. When you show mercy, you show respect for life. But if you can't respect *that,* we'll be forced to kill you!" I raged.

"Go ahead and take your best shot!" Cocone concluded the conversation. It was time to battle.

The five of us had made it too far to lose at the hands of these two blubbering idiots. We deserved better.

The five of us started charging at the two of them to signal the start of the battle, but Rodney teleported in front of Iris. She must have been concealing her anger, because she screamed at him before her eyes turned a shade of deep, angry red. She was more messed up about the concept of the war than I realized.

"Zonule!!" Iris shot out her signature attack of scarlet red disks from her eyes straight at Rodney. However, he sidestepped the attack with ease. The beam exploded behind him causing fierce winds from the aftermath.

"We won't let you take Jupiter," Iris raged. "Take th—"

Before she could call out her next move, Rodney punched her hard in the stomach and followed up with a jump kick to her chin. She was hurled up, and then kicked back down by the Eyebot dragon. She landed hard on the gravel and skidded away, out cold and outclassed. Then Pupil ran to her sister's aid and started to guard her, so Rodney took a break to watch us confront his brother.

Zephyr and I went to occupy a fight with Rodney while Zenon took care of Cocone.

"You do not want to mess with the two of us!" Zephyr bellowed before she charged at Rodney with me following close behind.

"Take this!" Zephyr put out a fist as if she was going to punch him, but then used the After-Image. When Rodney was looking around in confusion, I barraged him with a quick series of attacks, and then flew up to dodge his recovering kick. Then Zephyr came from behind him, and with every last ounce of her strength, she charged up her energy, then yelled, "Foveno Beam!!" She unleashed a golden beam of light right behind Rodney that quickly engulfed him in an explosion, and then Zephyr flew up to meet me.

"Do you think we got him?" she asked, trying to take her mind off of all her huffing.

"Not quite!" Rodney spat from behind us.

"B-but how did you—" Zephyr stuttered after we whipped around to face him.

"You'll find out soon!!" He disappeared, appeared right in front of her, and then wrapped his tail around her neck. After he was finished squeezing the air out of her, he did something very unexpected. He threw her up, jabbed his horn right through her stomach, scrapped her body off, and then threw her down to eat dirt. She lay limp and lifeless on the ground with Rodney wiping her excess flesh and blood off his silver horn.

"Y-you freak! Look what you've done to her!" I fiercely screamed, unable to control all of my anger.

"What was that about you saying you'd show the true power of zeal? You can't even save you friend!" the half dragon scoffed.

"Rrrh! The battle has just begun, you pompous fool!" I raged right before I charged at him. We were then locked in a battle of mirrored attacks. It seemed that we were evenly matched, but soon, he started to overpower me, and so my technique quickly became messed up and sloppy. Finally, he landed a fierce kick on my left cheek.

However, I wasn't about to give up. I quickly twisted back around to face him. This time, when he tried to kick me, I was able to use the After-Image to get behind him. Then, I drop-kicked his head as hard as I could, but it wasn't enough. That's when I decided to use the Slow Motion Technique and landed an ultrapowerful energy blast attack on him. I thought that it would knock him out for at least a couple of seconds, but somehow, he got back in front of me! I was too exhausted to move, and so he elbowed my forehead so hard that I was sent as fast as a rocket to the ground.

"It's time to end this battle!" Rodney bellowed. "Scatopike!!!" He fired an energy beam from the tip of his finger, which had incredible force behind it. I leaped up and ran to cover Zephyr, who was barely able to move. I deflected Rodney's attack with my spinning force field, but with great effort; I wouldn't able to deflect another attack for at least two more minutes.

When Rodney had immediately fired the same attack a

second time, that's when horror struck the depths of my soul; we were going to die! But then, Zenon fled from her battle with Cocone and came in front of Rodney's blast. She was battered and bloody, and taking into account the way she was holding her left arm with her right, it was broken from the battle.

"I won't let you hurt my friends!! Choroid Gun!!" she screamed before firing her most famous sparkling green attack out of her hand. The force from her energy attack collided directly with Rodney's.

Even though I was partly relived since that the same attack had once subdued me, this is an Eyerobis dragon we were talking about. Zenon herself knew that it was no use.

"Jadeleve, take Zephyr and get out of the way; I-I can't hold Rodney off for long!!" Zenon commanded, trying to tough out the pain from the amount of energy it was taking her to stand up.

"Right!" I conceded. I picked Zephyr up and flew a safe distance away. "But you can't win. He's too strong!!" I called.

"I know on a regular basis I wouldn't survive, but the force from my attack will decrease the power and the amount of damage his will do to me! Take care of Cocone!! I've got this; I have help!" Zenon screeched with great effort, and then I understood what she was saying. Pupil had fired her most powerful attack at Rodney from behind, which distracted him long enough for Zenon's beam to engulf him completely. It was awesome, and the attack exploded in his face! But then I realized that we'd left Iris alone to fight Cocone!

"You pets are getting on my nerves! I'll show you how helpless you really are!! Photopike!!" Cocone fired a brilliant array of light straight at Iris that looked like Rodney's attack. I might have called it beautiful if it wasn't meant to kill my seven-year-old sister!

I was about to put Zephyr down, fly up, and protect her, but Pupil beat me to the punch. She flew right in front of Cocone's beam and first marked her territory by stretching out her arms.

"Take this!" She fired one yellow beam of light from each of her pupils and met Cocone's attack with a fire blast like Aiondraes's. Of course, as expected, Cocone's attack sliced right through it, but Pupil and Iris had already disappeared by the time it reached where they used to be.

Then, out of nowhere, Pupil was caught flying straight to a stunned version of Cocone.

"This is what you get when you hurt Iris!!" she cried, charging up the energy for an attack. In the dawn of the night, the radiant energy floating around her made her look like an angel. It was simply dazzling.

"Take this; Sclera Blast!!" she cried before she fired a sparkling baby blue beam straight at Cocone, which he was able to dodge most of. However, Iris appeared behind him and started thrashing him with all the energy she possessed in her body. Before the dragon could recover, she finished her barrage with a weakly powered rainbow light attack. It was a perfectly executed double attack!

"Weak attacks like that will never defeat us!!" He flew right at Pupil and punched her down so hard her contact with the ground had made a crater. Somehow, it was the final straw for Zephyr, and she was back on her feet seconds after.

"How dare you!" she shrieked in anger and skyrocketed

off the ground. She tried to slam into Rodney, but he dodged, grabbed her by her black hair, and kneed her so hard in the stomach that blood gushed out of her mouth. Then the half Eyebot drop-kicked her head, making her plummet and slam back into the dirt next to Pupil. However, she, unlike my younger sister, was able to lift her head back up.

Just when I was about to move again, Zenon flew up to meet Cocone and Rodney. Zephyr was able to snap Pupil out of unconsciousness, and Iris was finally able to recover from Pupil's trashing. The Original Five were, more or less, back!

That's when Zenon said, "Zeph, let's do the Twin Attack on Cocone!"

"Right!" Zephyr agreed. She flew up over to Zenon so that they were side by side. They then combined their energies and chanted, "Twin Attack!" Zephyr and Zenon's attacks morphed together to make one incredibly powerful weapon, and it was aimed right at Cocone. However, even at the speed the blast was shot, Cocone used the After-Image to dodge. Who would've thought that he knew that? Wow, did everybody know the After-Image?

"Where'd he go?" Zenon frantically yelled. Zephyr was calm and shrewd enough to know where he was, but Zenon was a second too late to catch on. Cocone appeared behind her and cried, "I'm over here!" He clasped his hands together like he was about to hit a volleyball and smashed the combined force of his hands down right on her skull. It sent her falling downward blindingly fast. Then he teleported below her and punched hard between her stomach and her gut in the most excruciatingly painful way possible. Right after the blood stopped gushing from her mouth, he grabbed the neck her shirt and threw her down to the edge of Pupil's crater. I could immediately sense him charging energy for his finishing move.

"No, Cocone!! Don't do it; you'll regret it!!!" I warned.

Shrugging off my warning he yelled, "Maybe this will teach you not to mess with us!! Photopike!!!" Cocone fired his brilliant black and white (but certainly not pretty gray) light beam straight down at her. Too slow to react or do anything to stop it, the beam engulfed her entirely and exploded from the contact of the ground, and her.

"You fiend!! You killed my sister!!! How could you!!!?" Zephyr lamented. She genuinely wanted to know how anyone could be so heartless.

"It was easy, really, and now that you got me worked up, you and your friends will follow!" Like Rodney did to Zephyr, with blinding speed, Cocone flew up to Pupil and stabbed her with his horn. However, Cocone stabbed Pupil's shoulder.

"Owwwww!!!!" she cried in reaction to the amount of pain a seven-year-old girl wouldn't receive in ten lifetimes. Then he cruelly started twisting and turning his razor-sharp horn around inside her shoulder and laughed in spite of her cries of anguish.

"You stop that right now!!!" Zephyr charged at him and delivered a punch so fierce that it wedged his horn out of Pupil. In fact, she broke the tip off, making it useless, while I just floated there, frozen. My whole world was about to fall around me. In other words, I was in the depths of terror; these Beings were barely trying!

Pupil's eyes went white with unconsciousness just before

Zephyr took her in her arms. Then she tossed her to me to hold so she could keep fighting.

"How dare you break my horn!! For that, we'll kill you!!" Cocone screamed. He teleported behind Zephyr and bashed his shoulder into her back. However, Zephyr used the After-Image to dodge Rodney's incoming horn; it was a failed double attack. Rodney was too late to recover and flew straight at his brother with his sharp horns, and Cocone was forced to dodge.

"You anticipated our movements. Very nice, but this battle is far from over. By the time we're finished with you, there will be nothing left but your rotting corpses," Rodney spat.

"Yeah, I'm only hearing a bunch of talk," Zephyr retorted. Did she really not know what she was getting herself into?

Rodney charged at Zephyr with full speed, anxious to continue the battle. Caught off guard, he was able to deliver a greatly powered kick to her cheek, but then she bounced back with an elbow to his. Then they started a furious punching contest in which they exchanged blows repetitively; so it looked like they were tied, but it was obvious who was stronger.

"I guess it's time for me to stop fooling around," Rodney declared while Zephyr was tied up with the act of huffing.

"You think you'll be able to toss me aside like I'm nothing now? Well, think again!" Zephyr roared. She then charged toward Rodney with all the speed left in her body. However, he was now too fast for her with his full strength added to the equation. He sidestepped her attack, and then kneed her in the stomach. Then he took advantage of her vulnerable state and barraged the same exact spot where he jabbed her with his horn. With the added pain, blood started to gush out of her mouth and her stomach.

"Such a pathetic species you See-throughs are. You are soft and weak from the influence of human genetics," Rodney insulted while still kicking Zephyr around.

"T-there is one thing that we See-throughs have that you don't, and it's class! Notice how I didn't say 'you Eyerobis.' Do want to know why I didn't say that? I'm saying that we, us five, are not the same as you two, because we have class! I'm not grouping the whole Eyerobis race together as the bad guys because I believe that there are still Eyerobis out there with class; Eyerobis who aren't afraid to stand up for themselves. I know that there are Eyerobis out there that think that the four races can live together in peace and harmony and aren't afraid to say it. If you don't stop this now, you will cause your own destruction!" she exclaimed. She then desperately attempted to strike back at Rodney, but he was just too strong. He overwhelmed her quickly with several punches to the cheek and a kick to the stomach, which sent her hurtling toward the ground.

"What do you do now, you waste of space? We, the Eyerobis, are the superior race, and we will always rise on top. You low-life cretins deserve to rot in the dirt for all eternity!" Rodney spat as he hovered down to meet her.

"I've been waiting a long time to use this move; you'll be the first ever person I'll use it on." Zephyr caught Rodney off guard by recovering quickly. She crossed her arms in front of her and started to concentrate her soul energy, and then screamed, "Zephyr Wind!!!!" She uncrossed her arms and released a gust with a force unimaginable. The wind's speed was so high and sharp that when it made contact with Cocone and Rodney it opened up deep gashes all over their scaly bodies.

While Rodney was trying to overcome the pain, Zephyr flew back up, delivered a blinding-fast barrage to his face, and finished it with a hard kick to his gut.

"Y-you call that an attack? You fool!! All you've managed to do was make yourself the first to die on to-do list!" he hollered with a mix of laughter and rage in his voice which caused Zephyr to despair.

"Oh, boy . . ." was all she could say before Rodney jammed his remaining horn right through her, throwing her up the air, and then screaming, "Take this—Scatopike!!" He fired a brilliant beam of color out of his hand, engulfing Zephyr in the process. Through the beam's sight manipulation, it seemed as if her body was dissolving or evaporating right before the explosion, and all I could do was watch in horror. When the smoke cleared, she fell to the ground, lifeless.

"Zephyr!!!" I screamed, trying to keep my sanity.

"So much for that 'class'!" Rodney teased sarcastically.

I tried to reach out or feel for her life force, her soul energy, but it just wasn't there anymore. It was like it, just . . . just disappeared.

N-no. . . It-it can't be . . . I thought before I shuddered with sheer horror. I slowly hovered down and gently placed Pupil on the ground next to where Zephyr and Zenon lay, motionless, before Iris appeared next to me.

"Iris, if you can still fight, you should come up with me," I said softly.

"R-right," she answered, trying hard to contain her

sorrow and anger; her eyes were a mix of shades of red and orange. She was learning fast that we had to be strong in times like this.

We slowly hovered up to confront the two laughing Eyerobi dragons. Iris was about to lunge when I yelled, "Somehow, we will find the power to destroy you; it's just the natural law of physics."

"I'll give you points for not running away while Rodney was beating up your friends and family, but you didn't even lift a finger to help them. I have to deduct points for that, I'm sorry," Cocone laughed.

"The fact that they got in our way was a reason to kill them; that's the real natural law of physics. It's simple," Rodney chuckled.

"Please stop this! I swear we're on a mission to obtain power. We need to obtain power to be heard; to be noticed. We want to unite the Lands once more and live on a planet with equality. The girl you just killed told you that, but I guess it didn't penetrate through that thick skull of yours. If you don't get out of our way and stay out, I'll be forced to kill you!" I roared.

However, no matter how thoroughly I warned them, Cocone charged at us with blinding speed, jabbing Iris in the stomach with his horn as hard as he could. Then he did the same twisted thing Rodney did with Pupil: he twisted his horn inside her, cutting deeper and deeper into the flesh.

I tried my best to punch him, but he was too fast. He whipped me hard with his tail, and then wrapped it around me so I had a front-row seat of him torturing her.

After one minute of Cocone's horn being lodged inside her, Iris's irises started to grow gray with lifelessness; not her moonlight shining silver shade, but dull and boring gray. They got whiter and whiter as her energy drained faster and faster and water started to seep out of her eyes. Finally, he dislodged his horn and punched her down headfirst to the ground.

"Iris!!" I screamed with restrained rage. Why did I want to kill these things so bad? "Dang it! Recatus!!!"

I used the Recatus as a diversion, and then I activated the Slow Motion Technique. I teleported behind Cocone, and then kicked as hard as I possibly could in the back of the head, right into the veil of purple I unleashed.

Before he could recover, the Recatus engulfed his body and the slowdown time had diminished. However, being exhausted, I was too slow to dodge what was coming next. Rodney came from behind and opened a huge gash on my back from scraping his wings against me. Then he used his tail to tie my hands and legs up, immobilizing me. Finally, he delivered a barrage of unstoppable punches to my stomach, and then untied my hands.

I fell back and tried to recover, but the twins wouldn't let me rest. Cocone was battered and huffing, but he was still able to fight and reappeared behind me. The Eyerobis had got positioned perfectly with me between them, and then wildly fired their best attacks. I knew that I'd be too slow to dodge, so I deflected both of their attacks right back at them, but with the cost of losing precious energy.

Somehow, Cocone appeared right behind me again, stabbed me in the back with his horn, and then threw me down to eat dirt. I didn't know why he didn't just stab me in the head and kill me, but I wasn't about to point out his flaw. Unhealthy amounts of blood seeped out of the spot I was struck, nonetheless.

Anyway, the twin Eyebot dragons laughed down at me from where they were hovering in the sky, like they're superior, but they had no idea . . .

Wait! The Healing Herbs that Dracon gave us, I thought. *All I have to do is get them to the guys and revive them.*

With the energy I had left, I flew over to the crater everyone was conveniently lying around, while Cocone and Rodney were laughing their heads off. I fed one to Zenon first, flew over to where Zephyr was and gave her one, and then I took care of Pupil and Iris. Finally, I plopped the last one into my mouth before turning back to the twins.

"Cockiness is your only weakness. Unless you get rid of that, I'll always find a way to destroy you!" I roared up at them as the other members of the Original Five rose off the ground.

"It doesn't matter how many times you come back, because now that we're not holding back, this is going to go by a lot quicker! Can I do the honors, Cocone?" Rodney asked his brother, making me shiver with disgust.

"Be my guest!" Cocone bellowed, flying off to the side. Pupil and Iris went left to take on Rodney while Zenon, Zephyr, and I handled Cocone. Our forces were so uneven, I know.

"Take this!!!" Zenon shrieked as she tried to hit Cocone, but she couldn't even land a single attack.

"Is that the best you can do?" Cocone mocked as he fired

his Photopike Technique straight at her. However, Zenon was able to use the energy force field attack to deflect it, and then she disappeared using her Conjunctiva Expansion technique. Zephyr immediately took her place as the battle raged on. *We have to be tiring the Eyebots out by now, right?* I thought.

However, Cocone used his tail to beat up Zephyr with such destructive force that she started to cough blood again, which meant that my friends were so beat up that the herbs couldn't fully heal them.

"Stop it!!" I intervened by punching him away from her.

"If you want die first just say so!!" Cocone teased.

"You disgust me! Foveno Beam!!!" Zephyr screamed. I couldn't imagine where she got the energy to do that! Anyway, her beam completely swallowed him in an array of golden light. The smoke from the explosion may have covered Cocone's face, but not his laughter.

"A weak move like that will never do us in! You deserve to die!!" He plowed through the smoke and stabbed Zephyr with his horn in the same spot as before. Then he quickly dislodged it and slashed her down to the gravel as hard as he could with razor-sharp claws.

"Zephyr!! You'll pay for all the pain you've dealt to my sister!!!" Zenon bellowed as she charged at him. This time, Cocone bashed into her right side with his sharp wings, leaving a gaping, blood-filled wound in its place. Then, he flew up higher and danced around in the sky, making a full circle. With the added speed, he slammed into her stomach with his two fists and all his force, skyrocketing down with her attached to his hands. Finally, he cruelly bashed her body into the ground.

"Argh!!!" Zenon moaned in reaction to the pain of the damage done to her body. "I . . . I; we have to win for Jupiter! I won't give up!!! Choroid Gun!!!" Zenon screamed as she fired her green energy ray right out of her hand.

"Seriously!?" Cocone spat before he used his hand to swipe the beam away and direct it right back at her.

"I-I can't m-move . . ." Zenon whispered; she didn't have enough energy left already to use her energy force field. That's when I decided to deflect her blast again with my intentionally weak-powered energy beam. Zephyr was able to sneak up behind him and attack with her strongest move.

"Foveno!!" she cried.

"Recatus!" I bellowed, following up. Both collided with Cocone with our deadly aim.

"Gahhh!!" Cocone was left in pain and malice-induced anger. "You. Will. Pay!!! One hundred-fold!!!!" He somehow got behind Zephyr who was behind him and knocked her body aside with unfathomable force, hurtling her sideways for yards. She bashed into and through about six steel rock formations. Even after all the pain she was dealt she was still alive, but she could barely keep her eyes open.

Zenon tried to rush to help her twin, but was interrupted when Cocone dealt her the most gruesome thing possible. He delivered a kick to her stomach so powerful that his leg plowed right through it, making her cough up pints of blood. He dislodged his leg from her gut, kicked her up in the air by the chin, and then punched her a mere one hundred and fifty meters away. Then he left her to fall lifelessly again to the ground—this was the final turning point in the battle, and we weren't on the winning team.

"Uhhh . . . I-I," I stumbled in the face of death. Then my attention was grabbed when Pupil and Iris separately cried.

"Sclera Blast!!"

"Zonule!!" Pupil fired her baby blue gun, and Iris fired her enraged red straight at Rodney. The two beams connected and exploded in his face while making full contact. But Rodney was barely shaken, and when he emerged from the smoke, he punched both the twins with either fist. Finally, he slashed them down with his tail. When they fell to the ground, however, they were both able to get back up.

"Ha," Pupil attempted mockery, "is that all you—"

Cocone cut her off. He teleported behind her and attacked so hard that the force broke her back. He used his razor claws to plow through Iris and stabbed his horn through Pupil. Lastly, he concluded his assault cruelly by making his horn cut deeper into her flesh. Iris, who had just about had enough of these Eyebots, was forced to recover from the blow she was just dealt and save her sister. Her eyes started to get an angry reddish-silver tint to them.

"I'll break you in half!" she roared, jumped up, and then kicked Cocone's horn so hard it broke off. She carried that part of the horn that held her sister and dislodged it from her stomach. Finally, she stomped on that piece and started breaking it into tiny pieces. "I'm going to start small and work my way up!"

"Why you . . .!!!!" Cocone screamed furiously before he swatted her away with a hard elbow. Iris was still able to get up, but the contact from her fall broke her left leg.

Before she had time to blink, Cocone had wrapped his

tail around her face so she couldn't see. He then cruelly barraged her in her exposed state and threw her back on the ground. I watched in anger as my littlest sister (since she was five seconds younger then Pupil) shivered with pain, remorse, and worst of all: fear.

"I-I d-don't under-understand," Iris coughed. "W-why are you—?" but before she could finish her pain-coated question, Cocone kicked her away with concentrated energy in his leg, teleported to her again, and punched her down to the dust.

When Iris blacked out a second later, she was powerless to prevent Cocone from flying up to punish a bewildered Pupil who was still recovering from the horn that was lodged in her back. He grabbed her by her blue shirt collar, kneed her hard in the stomach, which expelled more blood, and then punched her back down to share a dish of dirt with her twin. Then both the Eyerobis turned their attention to Zephyr and me in disgust.

"It's a shame that you're all so pitifully weak! I thought that the sixth kick-off battle of our land of the See-through Invasion's debut would be more of a challenge, but I guess not!" Cocone mocked.

"How could you hurt our friends—wait, I think I've already asked that question. It's no use trying to get through to you; soon, I'll have to personally show you what you're getting yourself into. Anyway, what do you mean you're 'sixth' See-through Invasion battle?" I questioned.

"We're going to kill you here, so I guess telling you this information won't hurt. You see, across the land, we've been battling with the one called Xaphias. He's a very skilled warrior; much more skilled than you. We've been searching for the strongest fighters to take out first before the real invasion begins, and Xaphias was our fifth opponent. You guys would be our sixth in this war, so we thought the challenges would keep getting harder, but I guess not," Rodney further explained, and then sighed.

"Look, Jadeleve and I are the top dogs. If you want a challenge, come and get one!!" Zephyr screamed before she charged.

When she came in contact, Rodney attempted to whip her with his tail, but she was able to dodge it, grab his tail, take his leverage, and fling him away. She then started a punching match with Cocone, but was quickly overwhelmed from exhaustion. He was able to use her own force against her and wrap his tail around her neck. That's when I decided to jump in.

I cut half of his tail right off with the sharp force of an energy beam. Afterward, I incinerated the cut off piece of his tail with another attack. Zephyr was able to pull off the excess flesh from Cocone's tail from her neck and recovered at about the same time Rodney recovered; it was back to battling!

Cocone decided to start off the second round by striking Zephyr in the face with a series of hard kicks and punches, then slammed her up in the air. Rodney somehow escaped my sight, appeared from behind her, and punched her down. Finally, Cocone flew up to meet his brother so they could gloat together again.

"You're even weaker then the blonde! Our mission is to erase lower-class scum like you! People like you don't deserve to live!" Rodney roared.

"I can't believe you cut off my tail!" Cocone whined.

"I bet that's just what your mother says to you to let you sleep at night," Zephyr spat. "What you need to realize is that Jupiter doesn't need any more war, and we don't need purists like you thinking you're better than everyone else! We just have to put you in your place!"

"You are getting on our nerves! I hate when people get on my nerves; you must be annihilated!!" Rodney screamed as the two both got in some sort of stance for what had to be a lethal attack.

"Mesopike!!" Cocone and Rodney screamed at the same time. Together, they concentrated their energy and fused their powers. Together, they fired an energy beam with the force of which I've never felt! It was directed at who used to be my hated enemy, a nuisance, a peeve. However, Zephyr was now someone I looked to for comfort, someone I could respect. She was my rival, my adversary, and a friend.

I was about zip down and help Zephyr when she cried, "Zephyr Ice!!!!!!" She concentrated the same type of energy into her arms and released it like when she used the Zephyr Wind Attack earlier, except it was a different. She drew from a colder type of energy, a colder wind, and the blizzard came with ice spears too.

The Zephyr Ice Technique came in contact with the Mesopike, but it could only slow it down, making the force weaker. However, Zephyr knew her limitations, and she knew that she wouldn't be able to stop an attack of that caliber. She had meant to slow down the speed of the blast so she had time to fly out of harm's way without my help.

But Zephyr, even with all our training, was too slow to get out of the Eyebot's reach quick enough. Rodney was sly enough to follow Zephyr's movements and beat her down into the Mesopike's path again. I tried to cut off the beam's path by using the Recatus, but Cocone cut me off when he punched me in the face. I recovered quickly, but I didn't think Zephyr would ever recover from the pain she was faced with.

The Mesopike had made full contact with her and split open her stomach! The energy beam had just gone right through her; it was the most terrifying experience that I ever had!! And all I could do was watch helplessly.

When the smoke cleared up, it revealed to me a dying Zephyr, one which was beyond my help.

"Jadeleve," she coughed, "i-it's okay—" but before she could finish, Rodney came and kicked her once more, making her cough up even more blood.

"Zephyr!!" I cried as I tried to rush to her aid. But Cocone pushed me back with an energy blast without even looking, making it pierce right through me. Then he decided to tend to me as Rodney slowly killed Zephyr.

"Please, please, please, get out of my way. You don't know what you're about to get yourself into," I whispered as calmly as possible. *If I show mercy to these ones, maybe they'll have second thoughts about See-throughs!*

"Shut up!" Cocone interrupted. "I'm going to make you suffer!!!" He lunged in front of me. Then, he focused every single last once of energy into his leg and kicked me in my stomach with so much force, I was sure the impact broke almost every bone in my body. After the unstoppable pain got to me, his energy scattered around his body again.

He swept me up with a kick of unparalleled force to my chin, swatted me away with a fierce elbow to my hip, and broke the last of my bones that could still function in my body. I was catapulted and smashed into the same steel formations my comrades had collided with before. "Ahhh . . . (augh, huck)!" I moaned after I fell down from the dent in the formation that held me for a couple of seconds. Rocks made from steel fell all around me, forming what looked like a tomb.

The only two that could withstand the pain of the slaughter and get back up were Zephyr and I. She stood between the Eyerobis and me in a protective way.

With a muffled voice I shouted, "Z-Zephyr, I just can't do it; I can't end a life; we have to give up!"

"Are you kidding me!? After all we've been through, you're just going to dishonor Jupiter by backing down? Look, Jade, you have the power to help end this war! I'm just trying to buy you time! You better be ready to take my place after I get my fill! You need to show these fiends your true power!" Zephyr roared.

"Zephyr . . ."

"You sniveling barbarians expect to beat us with jokes? I can't believe these two are some of the newest descendants of the Dawn and Zeal family! A blemish we will soon erase," Rodney snubbed as he lifted his hand to attack.

"No, you don't!!!" With all her might, Zephyr lifted off the ground and head-butted Rodney right in the stomach. She looked back and yelled, "J-Jadeleve, I can't hold him off much longer; take the others and go! That is better than all of us dying!"

"Right!!" I stumbled to grab Pupil and Iris. I was about to fly over to grab Zenon when my attention was caught by the battle.

"Foveno Beam!!!!!" Zephyr yelled in a last-ditch effort to hold them off, but it didn't work. The damage that Rodney took was a waste because Cocone teleported behind Zephyr while she was distracted and punched her down in the dirt.

"Guhhhh . . ." Zephyr whined, finally beaten and out of power. I expected that Cocone would decide she had enough and come after me next, but I couldn't have been more wrong. He walked over to Zephyr and said, "What a pathetic waste of a soul!! I'll put you out of your misery!!!!" Confused at the very start, I quickly realized the cruelty he was about to unleash.

"W-wait, Rodney! It's over!! S-so stop, you'll live to regret it!!!" I screamed at levels of reason that had probably had never been shown in all of history. But I couldn't stand it anymore; I needed a cue; something to call the last straw, to completely obliterate these laughing buffoons!

"Die, scum!!!" Rodney stomped on her back, smashing right through it, and her eyes turned pure white. Using lightning speed, he kicked me back, grabbing the twins out of my hands. With concentrated energy in each of his hands, he formed two smaller versions of the Photopike Technique, and then viciously jabbed right through their bodies. I felt like the cord that was holding their force just cut after that. It was like they just disappeared; gone! Their spiritual energy was completely gone! Rodney threw them on a pile with Zephyr.

"P-please . . ." I wept, barely hanging on to awareness.

The last thing I saw before I fell unconscious was Cocone adding Zenon to the list of my dead comrades.

When I woke up, I could tell that I had only been out for about a couple seconds; otherwise, the twins would've killed me in my sleep. I could tell that it was around four thirty in the morning, so the sun would be in the sky very soon. Perfect.

"There's only one pest left!" Cocone fixed me with a death stare.

"You-you . . ." I stuttered.

"You *what*!?" Cocone mocked, smacking me with unbelievable force at the back of my head.

I skid on the floor until I met Rodney's feet. He didn't even give me a second to breathe before kicking me up in the air at my chin and hitting me down next to the pile of my dear friends' bodies. It was so aggravating how I had to watch my friends fall right in front of me and how I wasn't able to do a thing about it. How I had to witness helplessly my best friends' deaths at the cruel hands of these . . .

"Monsters . . ." I whispered.

"What!?" Rodney teasingly asked laughing alongside of his brother.

The truth was . . . that I did have the power to defeat the Eyebots, and it was finally time to bring it out. It was finally time to put my training to the test! I had mastered the stamina!

"I told you not to push me. I told you not to get in our way, but you just didn't listen! And now, I am going to kill you!! For the future of the Land of See-throughs! For the future of Jupiter!! I need to avenge my friends . . . I mean, you killed them, and you didn't even care . . . Well, I'll show you!! I'll show you the reality of my power—the ultimate power! The Power of Zeal!!!!!"

With an explosion effect following my threat, green energy started to swirl around my body. As the glowing, vibrant, and fanatic energy started to flow, my golden hair flowed as well. My power began to skyrocket, and I felt taller and stronger; free of my shackles. Finally, this was the true extent of my power; I felt more alive than ever in my entire life; I had complete control of the zeal! Now, it was time to use my power.

As my energy finally stopped growing, the sun rose up behind me, giving me light and confidence. I took one look back at my dead friends, a sharp reminder of what must be done. Lastly, I lunged at my enemies, taking one more step toward a brighter future.

The Power of Zeal

"AHHHHH!!!!" COCONE AND Rodney shrieked in pain as I kicked through both their stomachs at the same time. Rodney was able to get out of my grasp, but was helpless and could only watch his brother get beat up. He tried to punch me from behind, but I stepped out of the way at the last second, letting him bash into Cocone.

"I can't believe you two fell for that! That's the oldest trick in the book!" I laughed, charging at them once again. This time, they decided to make the first move and struck me square in the face simultaneously. They watched in triumph as I skidded away on the gravel.

"Take that!!" Rodney yelled in victory. Only pretending to get hurt and letting them hit me, I got up quickly without a scratch on me, well, except the ones that came from the earlier times of the battle.

"I know you guys have some sort of trick in store, so don't hold back!!" I roared, preparing myself for the big one.

"Ha-ha!! You are very smart, aren't you!? We still have a couple more surprises for you!" Cocone smugly laughed before they both lunged.

With blinding and cursory speed, Cocone and Rodney barraged me with what was their true power, and I'll tell you, I really got a load of it. Each strike had bone-shattering power held behind it, but luckily, right in the middle of the slaughter, I was able to recover and return every attack, punch for punch, right back at them, switching between kicking Cocone and punching Rodney. It would have been an endless loop, and I knew that they didn't have the stamina left to keep up with me.

"Enough!!" I cried as I blew them away with sheer energy, deciding to go after Cocone first. I super-kneed him on his forehead, and then kicked him at Rodney. Successfully, I forced their bodies into a devastating collision.

Before they recovered, I appeared behind them and grabbed Rodney's tail, immobilizing him. Then I swung him around a few times before throwing him at Cocone and making them bash into each other again.

"Why . . . you . . ." Cocone squeaked in a fit of rage. "Take this!!!" He fired a new technique, which looked like a fireball, right out of his hand. I was able to deflect it back at him, but Rodney came from behind and shocked me with electricity on my back, using a move similar to that of Dracon and Aiondraes.

While I was falling down from the force of that blow, Rodney followed up by kicking me farther away, square in the stomach. Caught completely off guard, I skidded away on the gravel, trying hard not to think about the pain.

"Y-you hit me with my own technique . . . Do you know how embarrassing that is!!!? Photopike!!!!" Cocone hollered before he fired his signature beam straight at me. Then, he decided to fire about fifty regular energy beams behind it, draining a lot of his energy. I was able get up and dodge the first beam, but all the others made full contact, engulfing me in an explosion of color. However, when the smoke cleared, I revealed to them that I was barely shaken from his hate-filled assault.

"Whatever you do is hopeless! I told you: I can't allow you to win!" I screamed, getting ready to finish our battle. But before I could deliver the big finish, Rodney came from behind me and used all his energy for one last powerful kick. And I couldn't believe it: The force of it had broken my right leg.

"Argh!" I cried with agony, falling to the floor.

"What a-are you going to do now!?" Rodney huffed and scowled.

My blood and rage pulsed as I scowled back at him in hatred. I didn't want to waste a life, no matter the cost, but I had no choice. I had to be the signal for the start to putting an end to this war.

But before I could act, Rodney appeared in front of me and kicked me up in the air, and then punched me back down with such grueling force I'm surprised no blood gushed out from my mouth.

"It's hopeless. No matter h-how much you beat me . . ." I stuttered, trying to stand up, but Rodney kicked me up in the air again, this time shouting, "Scatopike!!!!!" His ultimate attack swallowed once again, and it acted like an energy absorber, just like transflare. However, I wasn't having any more of this.

When the twins tried to assault me, I beat them down

again and again. Cocone tried to grab my hair, but I used the After-Image to get behind him, and then used it again to avoid Rodney kicking me from behind. Rodney ended up kicking his twin in the back, I elbowed the back of his head as hard as I could, and they both came crashing down again.

This time, I followed them down. I was able to dodge and evade every single one of their combined attacks. I was agile enough to get out of the way of their claws, deflect the power behind the strike, and use it against them or block it. Then I whipped around, triple-kicked Cocone in the face, jumped on top of his head to avoid Rodney's tail, and then used the energy force field to blow them away.

However, just like they did to me, I wasn't about to let them rest. First, I used my new energy slice technique, the same attack I used to cut off Cocone's tail, and cut off both their wings so they wouldn't be able to move correctly. Next, I used the slowdown technique, teleported in front of them, kicked all their teeth out of their mouths, and punched them back down onto the ground. Lastly, while they were on the ground, I struck relentlessly with a technique acquired awhile ago called the energy force technique. With this, I could use invisible energy to attack my opponents without even getting my hands dirty.

After my conscious told me that they had enough for now, I kicked them away, skidding across the hard gravel. I kept telling myself that I was using every single ounce of my current maximum power, but I wasn't proud to say I was still holding back. I needed one last, final push . . .

"I-If you attack us one more time, we will completely obliterate your friends' bodies!!" Cocone coughed, and then held up his hand toward the pile of bodies that had been my friends.

"No!! They deserved to remembered and buried after this battle!!!!" I screamed at the top of my lungs. I teleported in front of him and kicked him down with speeds that I never knew I could achieve. However, it was a wild mistake. Rodney, who was just a few meters away, attacked the body pile with all the speed and energy left in his body. Before I could react, his beam of white light exploded after its collision with solid matter: the flesh and blood of my dead friends and family.

"Heh-heh . . . f-fool," Cocone scoffed on the ground.

"I will never give up, and I will never forgive you for what you've done!!!!! It ends here!!!!!" I bellowed with finality. By focusing my energy into my hands, the space between my two palms filled up with purple, swirling, visible light. I could hear, well, not really hear, Rodney mutter something to Cocone before I started to chant and before I was about to explode.

Is this enough challenge for them? My mind raced. I had no regrets now.

"Double . . . Rec . . . aaa . . ."

First, the Eyerobis dragons nodded at each, and then they suddenly shot up into the air before finally shouting, "Twin lag explosion!!!!!!!!!" They fired two beams of light which merged together in an array of swirling light. Caught off guard, the blast made full contact, engulfing me into its explosion. With the devastated force, I fell to the ground in pain and agony. Could I really . . .

"Jadeleve, you can beat them. Just bring out that power we talked about," a familiar voice whispered into my head.

"Y-you, are you . . .!?" I shrieked in horror and wonder at the voice.

"Someone you haven't seen in a while. I'm also someone who's on a very tight schedule. Just destroy those freaks for the suffering of your friends and your sisters!!" the masculine voice roared before it receded within my mind.

I didn't care who the voice inside my head was, it was right! I had to avenge those who had died for me! I gathered up every last ounce of energy left in my body, which twisted and bent the clouds in the sky. Cocone and Rodney fired their Mesopike Technique right at me, also known as their combined attack. The partly black and white and partly colorful beam made full contact with my body, but the force didn't move me at all. I was in charge of my own will!

I let the dragons feel the depths of horror, and they deserved nothing less. They deserved justice!

"I told you before, I kept telling what you were getting yourself into, but you just wouldn't listen! Now, your time has come!!! For Jupiter!!" I started to fly straight toward them for the final time while starting up my chant once more.

But before I could finish again, Cocone and Rodney frantically screamed and fired the twin lag explosion in one last frantic attempt. However, it was over, finally and truly over! I dodged and kept coming, proudly. Their beam had missed its target, exploded against the ground, and left me with one final task.

"Ultimate, double Recatus!!!!!" I released the superconcentrated energy right from my control. In all its purple glory, it was directed right at them, but just when the attack was about make contact, they did the most twisted thing ever:

Cocone and Rodney both smirked! The purple explosion completely engulfed them as all three of us fell to the ground in exhaustion. I still had enough energy to stand and walk over to about ten feet in front of them while they had just enough energy to speak.

"Why . . . why a-are we s-still a-live?" Cocone asked me, coughing on his own blood.

"Heh-heh! It's-it's because I just couldn't bring myself to do it. I couldn't actually bring myself to kill. I still thought there might be a chance that you guys could change and tell the rest of the Eyebots that we can still live in harmony . . ." I explained.

"A-are you serious?! You fool!! We'd never settle for a truce. This is war, and you need to wake up and understand that. You truly are soft, aren't you?" Rodney laughed derisively.

"Do you have any idea what our plan was? The twin lag explosion detonates five minutes after it's fired at the ground. We figured that you'd be way too tired to move right after the battle, so we thought you would kill us and our final attack would ultimately incinerate you. It's a last-resort weapon! Ha! You fell for our trap! Even if you kill us now, you *still* lose!!" Cocone laughed.

"That's crazy!!! What about you guys!!?" I screeched, shocked.

"I guess we'll all die, but we're dying for a good cause. You are a waste of space! Neither of us can move!!" Rodney laughed.

They . . . we . . . this was the end?

It's just like Dracon said! I thought. *In a war like this, mercy only gets you killed. He kept trying to warn me, but I didn't listen! B-but . . . I couldn't let them win! I had to stay strong!! I would find a way!! For my family!!!*

"That's my girl. Your mother has taught you about me to the last detail. If you keep thinking like that, there will always be a way to win!" The same masculine voice in my head praised. Except . . . this time, it wasn't in my head. I didn't dare look up yet.

"Your sisters, Zenon and Zephyr, are all still alive; however, these guys won't be for long," the voice added.

"Si-si . . . Sil—" Cocone stuttered.

"Shhh, Cocone! I don't want her to know who I am until she looks up first! Jadeleve Amethyst Dawn, look up!"

I obeyed the voice and lifted my head off the ground to see a smiling man. He looked to be almost seven feet tall with a lean, muscular build, black combat boots, baggy pants, and a sleeveless gray shirt. He had tan skin, silver hair, and silver eyes.

"Uhhh . . ." was all I could say.

"Yep! The name's Silver, and I'm busting you guys out of here! We need to make this quick, though. I have a war to help fight in!" the man named Silver prompted.

"W-who are you? It can't be, or can it? Is that you, D-D-D-" I muttered.

"Oh, I guess you can call me Dad. Now come on, your quest is far from over," he brightly answered.

"Oh . . . WHAT!!?"

The Tales of New Beginnings

"D-D-D-DAD . . ." I stuttered. Suddenly I looked right into his silver eyes and registered the instinctual recognition. I easily brushed off the pain of the battle, got up, and cried, "Dad!!!!!!!!!" I definitely had exuberance to spare as I ran into his arms.

"It's been nearly eight years! How have you been?" he asked, unquestioningly embracing me.

"I've been better, Pop. Mom and Gold have already answered what you've been up to all this time, so I don't really have any questions, except, how did you get here?" I whispered.

"I teleported from Saturn to a place nearby here using this new technique I invented. I can basically convert the sun's energy into speed, direction, and space energy memory. I thought Gold had told you about before," Dad explained.

"Oh, I remember! He did mention that you invented a new ability like that back in June. Anyway, what are you doing back on Jupiter?" I asked.

"I anticipated this outcome in your fight with Cocone and Rodney. I thought you might not have the heart to kill them, so I came here to make sure that you, your sisters, and the others, were all safe," he replied.

"I'm sorry . . . I just didn't have the heart . . ." I sulked.

"It's okay for now, Jadeleve, but in this war, make sure you watch your back," Dad warned.

I spaced out for a second and put my birthday pendant around my neck again for the rare time that I needed extra comfort.

"That reminds me, I never got around to using the transceiver; I guess it's not for me," I sighed, pulling the black pad from my pocket.

"That's okay. I'll take it off your hands. Now let's wake up your friends before this bomb goes off." Dad straightened and walked over to the pile of bodies clustered about twenty meters away.

"Yo, Dad, I sensed that their spiritual energies were all completely gone before I decided that they were dead! That's strange; while they were on the ground, Rodney attacked them with another energy attack that looked like it made full contact. Why weren't they blown away from the force?" I questioned.

"All of that is my doing. Telepathically, I quickly told them how to completely cloak their energy so that they could trick you into thinking that they were dead. I knew that it would draw enough power and energy from you than you've displayed before. That power was what put them in their place, Jade. You stopped a foe not even Xaphias could defeat. Also, I was able to pinpoint the direct placement of their life forces and protect them with a roaming energy shield at the moment Rodney attacked them that time," Father further explained.

"Wow, the energy cloak, a roaming energy force field—can you teach me your new techniques?" I piped up.

"I'll have to do that later, because I really have to get back to the war. I just thought saving your lives was a good reason to take a little break, so I'll have to teach you later," Dad replied. "First, we have to get you to a safe place!"

After encouragement from Dad and I, the gang started to open their eyes. Zephyr was the first to speak.

"So the plan worked?" she laughed.

"Yes!" Dad answered cheerfully.

"I can't believe you put me through that! That was the most dreadful hour of my life!" I whined.

Consecutively, Zenon, Pupil, and Iris woke up soon after Zephyr.

"W-what happened, Jadel . . . Dad!!!!! You're my dad!!!! The legends are true!!!!!" Pupil screamed like she's never screamed before. She ran over and fixed Dad with a great big hug. Iris was speechless, but her eyes were colorful with all sorts of emotions, and she gave Dad her own squeeze.

"We finally beat the Eyebots!!!" I cheered.

"You only beat the scrubs, you fool!!" Cocone was trying hard not to cry.

"Silver!!? Xaphias hasn't heard from you in years! Welcome back!" Zenon greeted, amazed, ready to accept that this scenario wasn't a dream.

"Come on, guys! This place is set to explode any minute now because of a lag attack Cocone and Rodney used. I'll teleport you to the southern tip of the Laputa; that is your next destination, right?" Dad urged.

"Right, how did . . . I-I guess that's a stupid question,"

Pupil stuttered.

"The fighting back on Saturn is thicker than ever! If I don't get back soon, they'll break through our forces in a matter of weeks!! Everyone, hold hands!! We're leaving the twins behind!!" Dad roared.

"Just know, Silver!! We will never stop until every last being on this planet that is not 100 percent Eyebot is annihilated!!!" the Eyebot twins cried in unison as the negative energy levels in the ground rose. It was almost time for the detonation.

"Then I guess killing yourselves first was a great start!" I scowled. I enjoyed their wide-eyed expressions after my comment truly got through to them. I had finally penetrated their thick brains.

The five of us, the Original Five, had finally fulfilled Dad's wish and held hands. Lastly, at the instant before the detonation, we vanished, leaving Celestine County, along with Cocone and Rodney, in our wake.

"We're here!" Pupil yawned. The five of us first looked backward toward the Celestine Ocean, and then looked forward at Silver who was blocking the view of Alamos town.

"I'll be going now! Take care, you guys. Zephyr, Zenon, Pupil, Iris, and Jadeleve, you all have so much potential; you all have the power to make great changes. I've guided you as much as I can, so now it's up to you to make a difference in this war," Father whispered.

"Dad . . . I-I . . . you're right!" I stammered. Then I hugged him for a good long minute. We had the power . . .

"Bye, Dad! We'll make you and all of Jupiter proud!!" Iris beamed.

“That a girl! You bring home that Zeal Orb, and we still might have a chance! I’ll be watching . . . from above!” I waved right before he disappeared into thin air, just as mysteriously as he came.

That’s when I fixed my gaze directly on Zephyr and held her with a long, indescribable stare.

“You heard the man! Onward!” I roared.

“Since when did you call the shots?” Zephyr whined.

“Come on, Zephyr, everyone knows I’m stronger than you! It’s time to pick up the pace! If Cocone and Rodney are considered weak compared to the rest of the Eyebots, we’ve got to train hard,” I explained. I let a small sample of energy straight from the zeal spark visibly in front of everyone to show that I meant business, and then looked forward. And without another word, as the five of us started trotting calmly toward Alamos town, the sky started to look a little . . . brighter.

CPSIA information can be obtained at www.ICGtesting.com
Printed in the USA
BVOW031948180613

323651BV00001B/76/P